ROOKIE'S REGRET

TENNESSEE THUNDERBOLTS
BOOK 3

GINA AZZI

THREE CITIES PUBLISHING LLC

ONE
BEA

"THIS IS what you're supposed to want," I remind myself as I place down the quirky vase with my favorite succulent—echeveria—on the windowsill.

I fiddle with the group of succulents already resting there and gaze out the window. The street I spent most of my childhood biking down looks the exact same. The mailboxes are lined up in a neat row. Mrs. Hall's garden is in full bloom. Even the patch of sidewalk where my brother Bodhi and I pressed our palms in wet concrete is still there. My twelve-year-old handprint immortalized like a bee in amber.

"Bea?" my eldest brother Beau hollers from the foot of the stairs.

I sigh and square my shoulders. It was *my* decision to move back home after graduating from art school. I stretched it out as long as I could, finally earning my degree in early January.

Nevertheless, I offered. Living in our tiny corner of Tennessee is what I always said I wanted. In fact, if Beau and Bodhi hadn't supported my decision to attend art school in Nashville, I'd probably be right here, in this very room, gazing at the same street. Exactly as I am right now.

I move to the doorway. "Up here, unpacking!"

Beau's heavy footfalls sound on the stairs and I loiter in the doorway, waiting for my brother's strong, formidable frame to come into view.

He grins when he sees me. It's the same easygoing smile of my childhood but now, Beau's eyes are different. They're shaded in a disconnect, a distance I don't fully understand. Bodhi says war and time away from home does that to a man. Since Beau served two tours in Afghanistan as well as several embassy duties, I guess Bodhi's right.

"You settling in okay?" Beau asks, leaning against the opposite wall and crossing his arms over his chest.

"Just unpacking my plants."

The corner of my brother's mouth lifts. "You sure about this, Bea? You could have tried for a job in Boston or L.A. You didn't have to—"

"I *want* to be with Gran," I cut him off. I mean it too. After our parents were killed in a freak helicopter accident when I was nine, Gran took all five of us Turner kids in, and raised us as her own.

Now, she's nearing ninety and starting to slow down. After a close call that involved hairspray and the fire department, a near flood in the basement, and a fall that should have resulted in a broken hip, it's clear Gran can't be on her own.

With the twins, Brody and Blake, in California, and Bodhi making a real name for himself in Miami, it's my turn to be here. Beau has held things together since his honorable discharge from military service. Now, he's embraced his dream career, playing goalie in the NHL for the Tennessee Thunderbolts. My brothers have sacrificed years, career opportunities, and social lives to raise me along with Gran. It's time for me to step up and start taking care of my family, even if a small part of my heart yearns for something beyond the state lines.

"It's good to have you back, kid," Beau says.

"Nashville isn't that far away," I remind him.

Beau shrugs. "It feels different, knowing you're here. I can't tell you the peace of mind I have knowing you'll be looking after Gran."

"Are you all packed and ready to move to your bachelor pad?" I joke, knowing that Beau is desperate to have his own space. Between his massive career change and the PTSD that followed him home, he needs it. Gran's hovering over him has only exacerbated his anxiety.

The pinch between Beau's eyebrows deepens, another shadow passing through his gaze. I tilt my head, realizing how much my brother needed me to come home to watch over Gran.

For the first time since committing to this move, I feel better about it. Watching Beau struggle, to adjust to his new normal, to embrace his dream—playing in the NHL—come true, makes my heart hurt. Beau's always put our family, me, first. And now, it's my turn to be here for him.

After too much silence passes, I clear my throat and Beau's eyes jump to mine. He offers a sheepish grin and ducks his head.

"Yeah, I'm ready."

"Good." I pat his arm as I move to walk past him.

"I lined up a job for you."

I stop short as a streak of shame, a swell of pain, washes over me. Does he think my art career won't pan out? Does he think I can't hack it in my chosen path—pottery?

"Just for the time being," he quickly tacks on. "While you settle in with Gran..." He clears his throat. "While you plan for your pottery business, I figured this could tide you over. It's good to have a backup plan anyway."

"What is it?"

"Cupcakes," he says brightly, and I turn to face him. He smiles and my hurt evaporates. While Beau has always supported my decisions, his enthusiasm in my pottery aspirations is lukewarm. It's not that he doesn't believe in *me*, he always says, it's that he's a *realist* about what a pottery career entails. Deep down, I worry he thinks I'll fall short.

Since our parents passed, Beau has always looked out for me. It may not be in the way I want, but I don't doubt his intentions. He always has my best interests at heart.

"Cupcakes?"

"Selling cupcakes," he clarifies. "There's a pop-up shop at the arena—"

"The Honeycomb?" I interject, lifting an eyebrow. The name is hokey as hell.

Beau grins and for a beat, he looks like the brother I remember. The version of himself before Afghanistan and war. Before he and Celine broke up and shattered each other's hearts and trust.

"That's the one. But"—he leans forward conspiratorially and drops his voice—"there's talk that the team may be moving."

"Moving? Where to?"

Beau nods. "Relocating into the city center."

"Like…by the football stadium?" Everyone with a pulse knows the NFL team, Knoxville Coyotes, are the pride and joy of Southern football.

"Yeah." Beau looks excited. "Can you believe that? Hockey is gaining popularity here."

"Can they do that? Just move a team closer to the city?"

He lifts one shoulder. "One of the team owners, Torsten Hansen, and his wife Rielle, have deep pockets. They own oil fields in Norway."

"Wow." Imagine having that kind of wealth? I shake my head; the idea is laughable. If Beau hadn't enlisted, I wouldn't have had the funds for art school.

"Yeah. That kind of wealth makes the impossible seem possible."

"I guess. So, cupcakes?"

"Yeah. Primrose Sweets. It's an NHL institution."

"How so?"

Beau wraps an arm around my shoulders as we walk toward the stairs. "The owner, Noelle DiSanto, is married to Scott Reland, owner of the Boston Hawks. *And* she's the daughter of the New York Sharks team owner, Rick DiSanto."

"Jeez," I sigh out. "This is like…incestuous."

Beau laughs and the sound makes me smile. It's loud and uninhibited. The way it used to be. He pulls me close and kisses my temple before releasing me so we can descend the stairs. "Run with that idea. Now that you're back, don't get tangled up with a hockey player, Bea."

I give him a look over my shoulder.

"Or football player," he tacks on.

Then, I laugh. I laugh so hard that my auburn curls shake, and I pause on the stairs to clench the railing. "Beau!"

"What?" My brother gives me a stern look.

I shake my head and make it to the bottom step. "As if an athlete—*a professional athlete*—would ever want anything to do with me!" I move my hands up and down my frame as if that should settle it.

Beau's gaze hardens.

"Beau, I've got wild red, messy curls, and am usually covered in clay and dust. I haven't worn makeup since Celine nearly took my eyeball out with a mascara wand for the eighth-grade homecoming dance."

My brother's expression tightens at Celine's name, and I silently swear at myself. Beau doesn't know that his long-time ex-girlfriend-turned-Hollywood-movie-star and I still speak. I tried to tell him a handful of times, but he shot me down.

As the only female presence, save for Gran, in my life, Celine was a connection I couldn't sever. I needed her too much, relied on her too greatly. And, even now, after my brother broke her heart, she's never not showed up for me.

"You're beautiful, Bea." His voice is solemn, strong.

"I'm quirky," I correct him.

He pulls me in for another hug. "Lots of guys like quirky. Even the professional athlete kind." He releases me and fixes me with another look. "You need to be at the arena tomorrow at 10 AM. You're meeting with Noelle."

My mouth drops open as my hands fly to my unruly mane of hair. "The cupcake goddess/heiress?"

Beau chuckles. "I hear she's down-to-earth."

"You're feeding me to the vipers." I shake my head. "The cupcake goddess and a stadium overflowing with hockey players."

"Hey! I'm a hockey player."

"Yeah, but you don't overlook me."

"Trust me, Bea. No one can overlook you."

My eyebrow arches, sarcastic as hell. "Do you remember high school?"

Beau's expression softens. "You've changed since high school. You're all grown up now."

"Yeah," I say softly. "We all have."

Beau nods.

My family has been through hell and back. We've all changed.

"Bea! You hungry?" Gran calls.

Beau and I exchange a smile.

Well, maybe not Gran. She's still tough as nails and sweet as lemons. But God, I love her. I love my brothers too.

My family is the reason why I'm back, curtailing my thoughts about New York and LA and art. Instead, I'll settle back into my life in this quiet corner of Tennessee the way I was always meant to.

The way I used to want to when I was in high school, with a steady boyfriend and childhood friends. Before I moved to Nashville and my world opened to endless possibilities, *this* used to be more than enough. Now, I need to convince myself that it can be again. It will be.

"IT'S lovely to meet you, Beatrice," a beautiful woman with blonde ringlets and bright blue eyes greets me the following morning. How does she tame her curls?

Is it awkward if I ask? Probably, yes.

I shuffle back a step at her beauty, which is blinding. But her smile is warm and her cupcakes look like magic, so I force my hand to dart out and take hers as gracefully as I can manage. "You too. It's just Bea."

"Bea," she repeats, her smile widening. "I like it. This is my better half, Scott," she introduces me to the handsome man walking up beside us.

The corners of Scott's eyes crinkle when he smiles, and he looks much friendlier than the formidable hockey owner I was prepared for. "Great to meet you, Bea."

"You too. Thanks for considering me for this position."

"Are you kidding?" Noelle gestures toward the pop-up stand and I fall into step beside her. "You're overqualified. Beau said you've got some other projects in the works, and I heard about your Gran." Her expression turns sympathetic, but her eyes are devoid of pity, which I appreciate. "So, consider this as temporary or permanent as you like, but if you do decide to go in another direction, I need at least two weeks' notice."

"Of course," I agree, confused. I thought I was interviewing for this position. What kind of strings did my brother pull to get me this gig? I'm hardly qualified; I'm one of the most socially awkward, stumbling, and stunted twenty-three-year-olds on the planet. "What did Beau say about me?"

Alarm must redden my cheeks because Scott chuckles.

"That you want to open your own business. Pottery?" Noelle asks.

I nod, feeling a rush of gratitude toward Beau. Maybe he respects my decision after all?

"If you need any business advice," Scott cuts in, "she's the one to ask."

Now, Noelle's eyes hold a different type of sympathy, one rounded out in understanding. "Especially when your family's not one-hundred percent behind you."

Ah, maybe Beau isn't as supportive as I hoped.

I dip my head. "Thank you, Noelle. Scott." I gesture toward the pop-up stand. "I appreciate the opportunity. Please, tell me everything I need to know."

TWO
COLE

That's my first thought when I see the beautiful redhead in the arena's cupcake stand.

Her hair is fiery, tendrils of auburn and gold. Her eyes are a soft grey, like a raincloud. She's got this mixture of fierce and sweet that makes me stop and take notice.

She's gorgeous in the most unassuming of ways. Stooped over a box of cupcakes, placing them carefully into a display case, she carries herself like she hopes no one will notice her. Bent head, rounded shoulders, a slim frame. But then, an expression crosses her face, thoughtful and wistful, a glimpse of longing, and I don't know how anyone could *not* notice her. She wears her emotions like a neon sign on her forehead, open, honest, and so obvious, I want to laugh.

Because right now, she's looking up at Noelle DiSanto and Scott Reland, like a deer caught in headlights.

Ah, I'll admit, their titles are impressive. Intimidating even. But they're both smiling at the gorgeous redhead with friendly, encouraging looks.

The beauty shakes her head and Scott chuckles.

"Yo!" River Patton elbows me in the side. "Stop checking out the new piece of ass and focus."

I glare at my teammate, about to tell him just what I think about his calling a woman a piece of ass. But my words die when I note the teasing gleam in his eyes.

"You like the cupcake chick?" River presses.

I groan. "Cupcake chick isn't much better than piece of ass, Patton. The woman has a name."

"Which is?"

"I don't know."

"Yet," he decides. "You don't know *yet*. Want me to find out?" He strides toward the Primrose stand, his chest puffed out, his full-sleeve tattoos on display.

I grip his shoulder and halt him.

He laughs. "You like her."

"She's gorgeous."

He turns to check her out, his eyes studious. "In a weird, oddball kinda way."

"I like quirky," I defend her. Defend myself.

Patton snorts. "You would, Rookie. Come on, we're going to be late for practice."

I fall into step beside him as we move toward the locker room. "Since when do you care about being late?"

River's expression tightens. "Since Devon threatened to bench me."

I whistle through my teeth. Our team captain, Devon Hardt, didn't seem like a hard-ass when I first met him, but once he committed to the Bolts, he's made it his mission to whip our asses into shape. For River, that means chipping away at his attitude. For me, it means pushing me to be more assertive. To display leadership qualities I'd rather shirk away from. As much as I hate putting myself out there, I think Devon's leadership style is working. It's helped the team fall into sync, with each player pushing past our individual hang-ups to strengthen the team as a whole.

I pull my T-shirt away from my chest. Just the thought of confronting someone makes me feel itchy, like I'm going to break out in a rash.

"Wow!" Damien Barnes, our left wing, checks his watch obnoxiously as we enter the locker room. "On time and everything."

River flips him the bird, but I grin and open my locker door.

As I suit up for practice, my mind wanders to the woman I saw. I've been in Tennessee for eight months now and have yet to meet a woman that's made me do a double take.

Sure, I've checked women out from time to time. The beautiful ones that men can't help but notice. The sweet ones that cause you to smile when you see them. But not a woman that pulls a man up short because everything about her—looks, expressions, energy—intrigues. The skittish lioness captivates, and the funny thing is, I don't think she wants to. I think she'd prefer to blend into the background, shuffle along unnoticed.

Except I noticed her. So much so, that I'm now thinking, wondering, about her. Is she a recent college graduate, like me? Last May, I graduated from Michigan State and now, I'm kicking off this year as an NHL player with the Tennessee Thunderbolts.

Is she from Tennessee? Or a transplant? Does she have a boyfriend?

"Philips!" Beau Turner snaps me out of my thoughts.

"Huh?" I look up.

"Let's hustle." He gives me a weird look.

Nodding, I close my locker door and follow my team to the ice.

The second my skates glide onto the rink, the strange emotions I experienced in the locker room, déjà vu mixed with curiosity, fades into the background.

The ice, hockey, is my place. It clears my thoughts, eases

my mind, and calms my body all in one shot. It was my ticket out of a dead-end future and the one thing I place above everything else, save for my uncle Kirk and cousin Jamie. There's nothing like the freedom, the possibilities, the sheer hope I feel when I'm on the ice. Not the normal, everyday distractions and definitely not the pull of alcohol or women a lot of my college teammates lost themselves in.

Nope. After my parents passed from an accidental overdose, I swore off drugs. And trouble. I'll have a drink every now and then, indulge more on my birthday or holidays, but I don't lose control. I don't go overboard. I don't put myself in a position to lose anyone's respect.

Instead of repeating a pattern, I broke a cycle.

As such, I sure as hell don't give into distractions. Especially of the female variety.

If my parents' untimely death, and then, moving in with my uncle and cousin, taught me anything, it's to never lose focus. When you commit to something, you see it through. Whether that be a career, a friendship, or growing a family. That commitment means more than anything else in your life.

For me, it's always been hockey. As a kid, the sport gave me a place, a team, and then, a family, outside of my shitty household. I was gifted concerned coaches instead of my dad's backhands. Uncle Kirk took an additional part-time job to cover the costs of the sport I loved. Between hockey and my uncle, there were hot meals and cut up fruit, instead of the spoiled milk and questionable sliced bread my mom kept in the refrigerator. There was an abundance of warm sweats and hats over the too-small coats and holey socks stuffed in my closet. Uncle Kirk provided for me the way my parents should have. Hockey gave me everything else—confidence, an outlet, a social network.

After my parents' deaths, hockey became an escape for my pent-up anger and grief, a space to clear my head, and a band of brothers to see me through the worst of my survivor's guilt.

Living with my uncle and cousin gave me stability and a warm, loving home to rely on.

Given the hand I was dealt, I've been fortunate. Lucky. I never want to take that for granted. Which is why I haven't dated much. I haven't tangled up with drama, or trouble, or confrontation.

I keep my head down and commit to the game. To my routine. To the team.

And the only woman who will ever get me to change my priorities will be the woman I marry. One day. When the time is right.

Not as a rookie. Not with a short-term contract and a probable move. Not when I'm still literally and figuratively getting my skates underneath me.

I glide down the rink with a renewed focus on practice. With a hunger to improve my game, to show up for my team, to play the best season I'm capable of.

But when practice is finished and the team's left the locker room, I loiter for a moment too long. I hesitate and stall as my stomach growls in hunger.

Then, I go buy half a dozen cupcakes.

THE GUY CHATTING up my lioness is pissing me off. That's saying something because I'm an even-keeled guy. I rarely lose my temper, I don't hold grudges, and I shy away from drama.

But this dude, damn, this dude is one step away from fucking harassment.

"You didn't tell me you were back," he whines, crowding the beauty behind the counter.

"Jay, I'm working." She places a cupcake in a bag. "And this is my trial run so…" Her voice trails off, but her eyes are pleading as she passes a bag, stamped with the Primrose Sweets logo, to a stressed-out mother with a screaming toddler.

The pop-up shop is rarely open outside of game nights, but this month, the arena is hosting a hockey clinic for kids. It's some type of outreach program aimed at spreading knowledge and love for hockey to younger school kids who've been ingrained with a football appreciation since popping out of the womb.

Jay looks over his shoulder, his eyes scanning me. He gives me a stupid smirk. "Babe." He turns back to the redhead. "There's no one here."

Her pleading eyes meet mine and color with apology.

"Take your time," I tell her, crossing my arms over my chest. I shoot the man a dirty look.

The guy sighs and leans over the counter again. "Just, tell me you'll meet up with me later? We need to talk, Bea. It's been years and you owe me—"

"Okay, time's up," I cut in, changing my fucking mind. Because now, I know her name. Bea. It's simultaneously quirky and timeless, which I like. It suits her. And she doesn't owe him shit.

Bea offers a tight smile. "Please, Jay—"

"Promise me, Bea." His arm darts out and his hand snakes around her wrist.

Anger I rarely experience blazes through me. Not because he's touching her but because she winces from his touch, her eyes zeroing in on his hold.

"We'll talk," she agrees, spiking my frustration.

He gives a curt nod and walks away, giving me a hard look as he passes. Sad. I could knock him out with my left fist. And I'm a righty.

I step to the counter, noting how quiet the hallway is. The

clinic must have resumed sessions from the break and the team is long gone, headed out to lunch or home to greet girlfriends or the one-night stands who didn't get the message.

"Welcome to Primrose Sweets. What—" she sighs and blows out an exasperated breath. Some of her red curls blow away from her face and her grey eyes meet mine, boldly. "I'm sorry about that."

"Don't be."

"It was unprofessional."

"He's a douchebag." I rest an elbow on the countertop. "And he shouldn't have spoken to you like that."

She fiddles with a stack of napkins, nervous. "He's my ex-boyfriend."

"Having a hard time accepting the ex part of that?" I bite the inside of my mouth. Why the hell am I grilling this girl? I don't know her. And yet…I want to. There's something about her that intrigues me. The little showdown with the ex only heightened my curiosity when it should have, when in the past it *would* have, shut it down.

She shakes her head, her wild mane flowing. "No, we broke up years ago. It's just, I'm back in town now and…it's complicated."

"I understand." I say it because it's partly true. I understand complicated better than anyone, just not in the romantic sense. I've never been invested enough in a partner to blur lines. We're either casually hooking up, or we're strictly friends. But complicated in terms of family dynamics? In terms of big feelings and uncertainties? Well, yeah, that's my whole life so… "Can I get half a dozen cupcakes?"

She smiles and it hits me like a sucker punch. Her entire demeanor changes, blossoms, when she smiles. Her shyness diminishes, her fierceness softens, and she's just…radiant. "We have birthday cake, chocolate, and apple strudel left."

"I'll take two of each."

"All right," she says, placing the cupcakes in a little box. "Are you here for the clinic?"

I glance down the long hallway, note a group of boys who run to a water fountain. I open my mouth and suddenly, I don't want to tell her I'm a Bolts player.

It's silly because being a hockey player is the one thing my teammates always bank on to get a girl's interest. But I don't want this woman, Bea, to like me *because* I'm an athlete. I want her to like me because I'm me, regardless of my job title. "I'm around a lot," I offer a half response. "Are you working here full-time?"

"For now," she responds, just as cryptically.

I grin, and she smiles back and passes me the box.

"I'll be seeing you around, Bea."

"Okay..."

"Cole." I hold out a hand, balancing the cupcake box in my other palm.

"Cole," she repeats, shaking my hand. I like the way she says my name. I like the feel of her hand, long fingers and cool skin, in mine. She tells me the total, I tap my Apple Watch to pay, and still, she smiles. "Thanks for coming by Primrose."

"I'll see you tomorrow." Now that I know she's working here? I'll be eating cupcakes every damn day.

"Tomorrow?" Her brow furrows.

"Tomorrow," I confirm, turning away. I open the box and pull out a cupcake, taking a big bite. Damn, it's good.

Sweet and delectable.

Just like Bea.

THREE
BEA

I SIT up straighter when Jay's car, a rickety old Toyota his older brother bought when we were in middle school, stops in front of Gran's house. He slips out of the driver's seat, looking mostly the same as he did on graduation night.

He's a good-looking man. Tall, brown hair, laughing eyes, and a dimple in his left cheek. But he's not as trim as he was in high school. There's a tiredness that clings to the lines of his face now.

Life hasn't been easy for Jay Roads. We bonded over our mutual loss and grief. In fact, it's one of the reasons I trusted him as quickly as I had. He'd lost his mom to cancer the year before my parents were killed. Our mutual loss, coupled with the history of living in a small town, pushed us toward each other and until I left for Nashville, we remained a unit.

Jay owns all my firsts. I hold all his. There was a time when I envisioned us married and settled in the little house at the back of his dad's property, raising a brood of children. My hands would be caked with clay and his fingers rough from building furniture in his granddaddy's custom shop.

It was a simple dream, but it filled me with pride. With longing and nostalgia and hope. It made sense. I was so certain of my path until I went to art school. Until I met new people, made new friends, and learned of new opportunities. New York, L.A., Europe. Galleries and showcases and portfolios.

I shake my head, clearing it of what-could-have-been thoughts. I came home for Gran, for my brothers. Right now, that has to be enough.

Jay ascends the rickety porch steps and plops down into the rocking chair beside mine. We've sat in these exact chairs countless times. We'd watch dusk settle and the sun set. We'd listen to the birds and the crickets. We'd talk about the future we'd build, the family we'd create.

"How was your first day?" he asks.

I rock back in my chair. I used to feel peace when he was here, rocking beside me. Why does it now feel stilted? Unfulfilling? More of a burden than a blessing? Is it Jay and the shadowy memories of high school? Is it coming back home? Is it having to press pause on the other life I dreamed up? The one my heart still yearns for.

"Good," I admit. "It's just temporary. As I settle in with Gran. Get things going for my shop."

"You still set on that?" I feel his gaze on the side of my face, but I don't meet his eyes. I don't want to look at one more person as they tell me my dream is farfetched. That potters don't make any money. That I need to do something with more stability.

"I am."

He clears his throat, but I'm grateful when he doesn't say anything else. Until, "But you're back for good?"

Am I? I roll my lips together. As far as my family is concerned, I'm back for good. I'm taking care of Gran. I'm settling back into my old routine, my old life. How can I bring up New York? Or any of the opportunities and experiences that shimmer just outside of my world, a different reality but still within reach?

My throat burns as I force out a confirmation. "Yes."

Jay's hand covers mine where it rests on the armrest, and I flinch at the contact. He tightens his grip. "Good. We can be us again, Bea. Don't you miss that? Don't you miss *me*?"

Pain sears through me at the hurt, the hope, in his tone. Jay is a good guy. For years, he was my constant. I hate that my moving away, moving on, affected him as deeply as it has. But my feelings for him aren't what they once were. Nothing is as it used to be and yet…here I am.

"I miss what was, Jay. Sometimes, sure I do. But"—I force myself to turn my head and look at him—"things are different now. I'm different."

"But you're here."

"I know," I concede. "But I don't want the same things I used to."

His mouth twists, disappointment filling his face. "You don't want a husband and family anymore?"

I shrug. "One day, I guess. But I'm twenty-three."

"We used to talk about marrying our senior year of high school."

I tug my hand out from under his. "But we're not the same people we were in high school."

"We're not that different, Bea. You don't change who you are in four years."

Except I have. I study Jay, wondering how I can explain to him all I've learned, all I've done. Internships and a trip to New York City. A roommate whose mom is a famous painter. Discussions about expression and movement that lasted until sunrise.

My entire world opened when I moved to Nashville. It's not far away and yet, my bubble was vastly different than here. Would Jay understand? Does he want to?

"I just got back, Jay. I'm settling in."

He sighs. "You need time, fine. I'm not going anywhere, Bea. I waited for you, for this." His smile doesn't reach his eyes. "We're supposed to be together. You'll see. Tell Gran I said hello."

He lopes off the porch and back to his car. I watch him drive away. I wait for the sun to dip below the horizon, for the sky to darken, for the cool night breeze to kick up. I pull my sweater tighter, a shiver rolling over my shoulders.

"Bea?" Gran calls. "Are you hungry?"

I go inside and try to embrace my new life. But it's hard when it feels more like an echo of what was instead of a cheer of what could be.

BEAU MOVES TO KNOXVILLE. Even though his commute isn't long, only forty minutes, knowing he's not in the house changes things. He clings to the distance, the space he desperately needs, and Gran and I give it to him.

Of course, I still see my brother at The Honeycomb but there, he's with his team and I don't want to appear the pestering, needy little sister.

Instead, I settle into my new routine. Breakfast with Gran. Laundry and cleaning. Meal prep and filling her pill box with her necessary medications. This month, I'm at the arena during the hockey clinic hours, bagging sweet treats for sweaty, enthusiastic boys and girls. On game days, I open the pop-up shop early, setting everything up for the rush.

On regular days, the hours pass slowly. I thumb through design magazines or read one of Gran's paperbacks, a cozy mystery, a historical romance, or a classic.

Within two weeks, the bright spot of my day is Cole. I find myself looking forward to his stopping by the stand. He comes every day, the way he promised.

Over the last few days, he brings along a joke. A corny, awful joke that is so not funny, we find ourselves laughing loudly at it. His blue eyes crinkle when he smiles and the lines in his forehead ripple with his laughter.

Even though Cole looks like a linebacker, he's got the disposition of a teddy bear. He couldn't be more different than Jay, and as my conversations with him grow longer, I realize how much I like that about him. His easygoing outlook, his friendly smile, is refreshing.

"What do you call a fake noodle?" he asks on Monday morning, dropping his elbows to the top of the counter.

Instead of leaning back, I lean closer, wanting to erase the space between us. I'm drawn to Cole for reasons I don't fully understand. He's not my usual type, which tends to be artistic and moody. He's nothing like Jay, more memory than reality at this point.

But his cologne is intoxicating, his personality captivating, and his looks—huge and overbearing with a smile that effortlessly charms—are downright hot.

"What?" I ask, tilting my head to the side.

Cole's eyes hold mine, filled with amusement. "An impasta!"

I snort and his smile widens. Our eyes hold, our mouths twitch, and then, we both erupt in laughter.

"That's the worst one yet," I tell him.

"You're laughing." He points at me.

"True," I concede. "But you need new material."

Cole shrugs, his eyes tracking me as I fill a box with four cupcakes. Sliding it across the counter, I ask, "What's on the agenda for today?"

"Just practice."

"Practice?" I lift an eyebrow. He looks like an athlete, but I've never seen him with the hockey team, horsing around as they leave the locker room after practice. I've never heard my brother mention him in passing the way he has Damien Barnes and Devon Hardt.

Cole's cheeks redden and he nods. "I have a question for you."

I grin. "A question or a joke?"

Cole presses his lips together, as if trying to contain a chuckle.

I roll my eyes. "I don't know why the cupcake went to the doctor."

Cole frowns. "Because he was feeling crummy."

I groan. "I asked for that."

"You really did. Practically begged for it."

I snicker.

"But it was a question, not a joke."

"What's your question?"

He straightens, his demeanor shifting from playful to serious. As he does, my heart rate ticks up. "If I ask you out for dinner, would that be presumptuous?"

My hands tingle as nerves ping around my body. Cole, the teller of bad jokes and the best part of my monotonous days, wants to take me to dinner.

"Ah, too forward," he decides by my silence. Before I can correct him by explaining my surprise, my excitement—guys like him don't ask girls like me out for dinner—he amends his offer. "Have lunch with me, Bea? Or coffee? Just, give me some of your time outside of here." He taps the countertop.

"Okay. I, yes," I stammer. "Lunch."

Cole smiles and I feel it, his delight, down to my toes. It's thrilling, to know that I can be a bright spot for him too. "Lunch," he confirms. "Tomorrow?"

"Two PM. I'm off at two since there's no game."

"I'll pick you up here."

I wrinkle my nose. "Can I go home and shower first?"

Cole laughs. "Of course."

"I'll meet you—"

"I'll come get you, Bea. Here." He passes me his cell phone. "Give me your number and I'll message you. Then, please send me your address and let me do this the right way."

"The right way?" I ask, saving my number before passing his phone back.

"Like a gentleman." He shakes his phone at me while I hear mine buzz in my purse. "That's my number."

Melt. I melt.

My brothers will tell you I'm old-fashioned. They always mean it in a boring, predictable way. The way that made me lame and no fun. I'd rather make a vase than stay out late. I prefer black and white films to whatever is trending in Hollywood, save for Celine's films. I love the scent of paperback books and getting lost in libraries.

They thought I'd settle down with Jay and tend a small house on a patch of family land while raising a brood. They didn't love that idea, mainly because they didn't care for Jay. But still, they had to push me to attend art school and move to Nashville.

Maybe, in some ways, they're right. I am old-fashioned. An old soul.

But not in the ways they think. I want to be courted and sought after. I want to be desired and challenged. I want to be with a gentleman. One who goes out of his way to impress me.

I smile. "Okay. I'll text you my address."

"And I'll pick you up at..."

"Three thirty."

Cole grasps the box of cupcakes. "I don't know how many of these I can keep consuming."

I laugh.

He winks and it's as silly as it is endearing. "Tomorrow at three thirty."

I watch as he walks away. My fingertips tingle, the way they do when I need to create. Butterflies release in my chest and my stomach tightens. For the first time in years, I feel the delightful mixture of excitement and nerves about a guy.

It's only been two weeks and yet, on some level, it feels like my connection with Cole is deeper than the one I share with high school friends who've known me for years.

As Jay blows up my phone and my friends from high school ask if I want to get high in the same parking lots we used to cruise through five years ago, I can't help but feel that I don't belong anymore. Except for Cole.

We talk about our current lives. Living in Knoxville and travel (he recently checked out the Gustav Klimt immersive experience when the team played Toronto). We discuss what we're reading (Rupi Kaur for me and *Patron Saints of Nothing* by Randy Ribay for Cole) and music we love (we both like Dean Lewis). We share cupcakes and Cole listens as I describe a foreign film I watched the night before—most recently *Caramel*. He once spent half an hour trying to convince me to read *Fear and Loathing in Las Vegas* by Hunter S. Thompson. I finally acquiesced and went to the library on my way home to Gran's.

Cole's presence provides a flicker of hope, of excitement, on days that already feel too routine.

FOUR
COLE

BEA'S HOUSE holds a nostalgic vibe that fits her perfectly. It's a Victorian-looking home, complete with a wraparound porch and rocking chairs. It's got this Southern throwback charm with a hint of necessary upkeep that speaks to a well-loved, well-lived-in home.

I stand at the edge of the driveway for a moment, admiring the picturesque scene of an old home, a tire swing, and enough grass for a kid to roam and adventure. I can see my lioness here, playing and growing and kicking up mischief.

I walk toward the house slowly, wondering how Bea grew up. Does she have siblings? Did her mom make home-cooked meals? Did her dad mow the lawn on Saturday mornings? Maybe they had family game nights and watched movies under the stars, with a projector playing the film on the side of the house?

The haunting sense of longing, almost a phantom pain, rolls through me. After my parents passed, I had a great upbringing with Uncle Kirk and Jamie. In fact, they provided me with the stability, discipline, and unconditional love that many in my position wouldn't have access to.

Still, I can't help but wonder what it would be like to grow up in a big house like this. One with endless land to explore, tall trees to read under, and have it bustle with brothers and sisters or neighborhood friends.

"Why, aren't you handsome." A voice rings out as I approach the first step.

Turning, I draw back as I spot an elderly woman sitting on a porch swing in the corner, hidden from view by a large Weeping willow tree. A crocheted shawl wraps around her shoulders and a blanket rests on her lap. "Sorry, ma'am, I didn't see you sitting there. I didn't mean to startle you."

"Psh." She flicks a dismissive wrist. "You couldn't startle me, boy. I've got the ears of an elephant."

I smile, trying to place her. I'm almost certain I've seen her before. The lines in her face are deep with age but also edged with laughter. Humor lights her eyes even though she tries to look stern.

"Picking up Beatrice, are you?"

Beatrice. It makes sense that my old soul would have a traditional name. In my mind, she's Bea, but Beatrice suits her too.

"I am." I lean closer and extend a hand. "I'm Cole. Cole Philips."

"We've met." Her tone is dry, unimpressed.

I grin. "I thought so."

She arches an eyebrow, waiting for me to continue. When I don't, she sighs, but I spot the laughter lurking underneath her feigned frustration. "You play for the Bolts."

I narrow my gaze. "I do."

"You're friends with my grandson."

Surprise rips through me and I rock back on my heels.

The elderly woman chuckles. "You didn't know?"

"Know what?" Bea asks, pushing open the screen door and appearing on the porch like an apparition.

I turn toward her and freeze. "You look beautiful." The

words drop from my mouth, bold and brash. In her Primrose Sweets T-shirt, with icing on her fingers, and a messy bun, Bea is gorgeous.

But right now, with auburn curls wild around her face, her grey eyes popping with mascara, and a simple, long-sleeved floral dress hugging her curves and cowgirl boots adding an edge, she's breathtaking. Otherworldly. Whimsical and romantic and—what the hell is happening to me?

"Thank you." She blushes.

The elderly woman behind me, I assume her grandmother, barks a laugh. "Beau and Cole are teammates," she announces, solving the riddle.

Bea's mouth drops open. My brow furrows. I turn back toward—"Gran?"

Gran's eyes twinkle before she tips her head back and laughs. She laughs like it's been eons since she's had the pleasure to do so, as if not much excites her these days.

Nodding, Gran continues. "Yes, Rookie. It's me."

"I knew we've met," I mumble.

"It was your birthday dinner," Gran confirms.

Bea moves toward my side. "Wait a minute…you know Beau?"

"Very well," I admit, half in shock, half miserable with the truth that—"You're Beau's baby sister."

Bea wrinkles her nose. "Hardly a baby."

"The youngest of five," Gran cuts in. "Four older brothers."

"You have four older brothers?" I wheeze out.

Bea's lips pinch. "Is that a prob—"

"You must have had the most amazing Christmas mornings," I muse, looking out over the yard with a new vision unfolding before me. Kickball tournaments and manhunt. Catching fireflies and running lemonade stands. Maybe they ran a car wash instead? For school fundraising?

Gran laughs again. "They were something else." She

pushes to her feet and both Bea and I reach out to steady her. She smacks our hands away like they're pesty gnats. "I'm fine, the both of you. It's getting too cold to sit out here much longer. Have fun on your date. Don't keep her out too late, Rookie." Gran elbows me as she passes, her laughter flowing over the porch long after the screen door bangs closed behind her.

"Why didn't you tell me you play for the Bolts?" Bea asks, her tone borderline accusatory.

I shrug. "Because I like you."

"Huh?" Her grey eyes narrow.

Jamie tells me I'm honest to a fault. Right now is no different. "I wanted to get to know you, for you to like me, as me. Not because I play hockey."

Her expression softens. "Do I look like the kind of girl who would like you because you play hockey?"

"No," I admit.

Her face falls.

"You look like the kind of girl who would *not* like me because I play hockey."

She grins. "There may be a kernel of truth to that."

"Just a kernel?"

Her grin widens. "Beau's my brother."

"Beau's gonna kick my ass."

Bea bites the corner of her mouth and my gaze zeroes in. I wish it didn't look so sexy. I wish I didn't find her so damn intriguing. I wish a lot of things but not too hard because… most of all, I wish I can have a shot with her. "You worried about that, Rookie?"

I shake my head. "I've had my ass handed to me before."

Bea chuckles, the sound light. "You still want to go to lunch?"

"Of course." Does she think I'd ditch her just because of her who her brother is? While it's not ideal, I'd rather Beau kick my ass than miss out on spending time with Bea. I hold out my hand. "It's just lunch," I remind her when she hesitates.

Bea releases a shaky breath and nods. Then, she places her hand in mine. "Right. Just lunch."

I'M A LIAR. A big, deluded liar.

Because lunch with Bea isn't just lunch. It's a hint at what could be. It's a tease of the life I always wanted with the right woman. The kind of woman I wish for.

It's a hell of a lot more than tacos and guacamole.

"I can't believe with everything we've talked about this hasn't come up, but you're an artist." I dunk a chip in guacamole before popping it into my mouth. "What medium?"

Surprise flickers across Bea's face. "Pottery. Mostly clay. I make vases. Some bowls and serving platters."

"That's awesome."

"You really think so? You're a professional athlete."

"Who followed my passion," I remind her, pointing to the dry clay under her fingernails. "Anyone who doesn't give up on their dream is awesome."

Bea smiles before sighing. "Except I'm currently selling cupcakes."

"Nah, that's a means to an end and you know it."

"I want to open my own business."

"So do it." I dunk another chip and hold it out to her.

She takes it and our fingers brush. Skin and heat and dried clay. It shouldn't feel as significant a moment as it does.

"What's holding you back?" I press when she doesn't respond.

"Lots of things." Her expression turns thoughtful, introspective. "I'm here to care for Gran."

I nod, having put the pieces of that puzzle together. A few months ago, Beau brought Gran to my birthday dinner after she nearly burned the house down. I know my teammate's been having a hard time balancing hockey with being a primary caregiver to an aging grandparent. He couldn't wait for his sister to finish school and move back home.

Except now that she's here, I'm getting the impression she doesn't want to stay forever. Opening a business usually means putting down roots.

"I'd never leave her," she adds.

"I know," I say. Even though I hardly know her, I know she means it. Bea doesn't strike me as the kind of woman who doesn't keep her word. She seems more like the kind of woman who would uphold any promise, even at her own detriment.

"I don't want to let my brothers down either, especially Beau." She shrugs and takes a bite of beans and rice. "I love sculpting. And I know I want to work for myself. One day. I just don't know if it's the right time."

"I hear that. Just don't wait too long. Anything worth taking a risk on rarely, if ever, comes at a good time."

She lifts her eyebrows. "Playing professional hockey didn't come at the right time for you?"

I think back to my parents' overdose. To the hockey tournament I was at, three states over, while they took their last breaths. In some ways, hockey was always a reprieve for me. An outlet.

In others, it seemed like a curse.

"Not the way you think." I polish off my taco and lean back in my seat. "You can always keep your day job, Bea. But don't lose sight of your passion. Not for anything or anyone."

She watches me for a long moment, her gaze shrouded in curiosity. I wait for her questions. They don't come. Instead, she takes another bite of her lunch and asks, "Have you watched any good movies lately?"

I'm not sure if I'm relieved or disappointed that she didn't ask the questions whirring in her mind. I never open up about my family. But with her, I'd be willing to wade in.

For Bea, I'm already bending my rules. It's only natural to assume that breaking them comes next.

BEA

I STIFLE a groan when I see the hunched figure, clad in a baggy hoodie, sitting on the top step of Gran's porch. Cole notices Jay the same moment I do because he draws in a sharp breath.

"The ex," he comments.

"Yep," I say, feeling weird. It's not like I did anything to encourage Jay seeking me out, but him being here, right now, with me returning from a date with Cole feels wrong. Awkward.

"You okay with that?" Cole's voice is curious but controlled.

I look at him, noting the tightness of his jaw, the grip he maintains on the steering wheel. His blue eyes are devoid of judgement when they meet mine.

I let out a slow breath. "There's a lot of history there." I turn back to Gran's house. Jay is standing now, his hands balled in fists at his sides, a scowl twisting his mouth.

Cole's deep blue eyes scan my face, as if looking for reassurance. "You'd tell me if you weren't good, right, Bea?"

With four older brothers, feeling protected isn't new, but coming from Cole, it's different. My brothers have always looked out for me. But I've never felt the protective and concerned edge from a man like Cole. He's clearly worried about me because on some level, he cares. The realization sends a thrill down my spine.

"I'm good, Cole." My hand grips the door latch. "Thank you for lunch. I…" I pause, biting my bottom lip. "I had fun."

He grins and his hand loosens its grip, sliding across the top of the steering wheel. "You say it like you're surprised."

I shrug, blushing. "It was refreshing. You're… unexpected."

His eyes twinkle, amused and something more. Something deeper. "What is a flower's favorite kind of pickle?"

I roll my eyes, enjoying his jokes more than I should. "What?"

"A daffo-dill."

I groan, Cole laughs, and on the porch, Jay simmers.

"I better go." I tip my head toward the porch, tempering my laughter.

Cole's jaw ticks with frustration. "All right. See you tomorrow, lioness."

"What?" I whip my neck back toward him.

"You're the quietest type of fierce I've ever encountered. Go easy on him…" His gaze flits back to Jay. "But not too easy."

I stare at Cole for a beat until our eyes meet. Understanding mixed with annoyance flares in his gaze. As much as he can't stand Jay coming around, he's not inserting himself into a situation he doesn't understand.

His respect for me, for my decision, makes me like him even more. "I'll see you around, Cole."

"Tomorrow, Bea."

"Tomorrow." I climb out of his car and close the door behind me.

I walk toward the porch, frowning at Jay and the daggers he's sending Cole's way.

"What are you doing here?" I ask.

Jay ignores me, keeping his eyes trained on Cole. Sighing, I turn around and lift a hand to Cole. It's only after his eyes meet mine, after he assesses I really am okay, that he beeps his horn before backing out of Gran's driveway.

Jay seethes for a long moment before sitting down on the step. His cool eyes cut to me. "You dating him or something?"

"Or something," I offer, not sure what I'm doing with Cole. But I like it. I like him, even though I shouldn't.

He's my brother's teammate. He's a professional hockey player. He's not sticking around.

I take in Gran's house. The porch needs a fresh coat of paint. The screen door hinges need some WD-40. The mailbox is rusty.

I sigh. I'm not going anywhere.

I take the step below Jay and wait for him to tell me why he's here. What does he want from me?

"You're not giving us a chance." His voice is quiet, laced with hurt.

"There is no us," I say gently.

Jay's expression hardens. "There should be."

"Things are different now. I need you to understand that."

"Because you met a city boy? A fancy, rich hockey player?"

"Because I changed. I grew up." I press a hand to the center of my chest, trying to explain myself in a way that won't hurt Jay.

Jay scoffs. "And I didn't?"

"We grew in different ways," I amend.

Jay shakes his head, jumping to his feet. The movement is sudden and unexpected. It causes me to rear back and bump my head on the railing behind me.

"Ouch." I rub at the spot.

Jay narrows his eyes. "You okay?"

"Yeah." I drop my hand and shuffle to my feet. "I don't want the same things I used to, Jay."

"But you're staying," he murmurs, as if trying to convince himself. His eyebrows dip together. "What else are you going to do if you stay?"

His question, while valid, hurts. Because I don't know. Because I'm not sure I *want* to stay.

"Sculpt," I respond, my palms suddenly tingling for the feel of clay. For the cathartic movement of creating and shaping. Of bringing something into existence and breathing life into dust.

Jay shakes his head again, bounding down the steps. "You need space. Time."

"Nothing's going to change," I say, my voice firmer than it was a minute ago. Why isn't he understanding what I'm saying? Why does he think I don't know my own mind?

"We'll see, Bea." He delivers it like a challenge, which causes my hackles to rise. "When fancy boy is traded to a new, better team, and leaves you without a second glance, we'll see."

"You don't know him, Jay," I retort, my temper igniting.

He snickers. "Neither do you." Jay turns, lifting a hand in farewell, and stomps back to his car, having the same type of tantrum from our high school years. Except now, the nervousness and stress that used to fill my limbs doesn't come. Instead, his behavior pisses me off.

I sigh and watch as his car blows a cloud of dust as he speeds down the road. Then, I turn and head toward the shed behind the house. It's my space to create and sculpt. It's my slice of peace, a place I can get lost, let my mind wander and my hands work.

I shut the door behind me, don an old green apron, flip on some music, and set to work.

Slowly, my anger at Jay, my curiosity for Cole, my confusion and uncertainty fades away. It's just my even breathing, the wet clay that begins to take shape beneath my hands, and the solitude of the moment.

I don't need anything but this. My passion, just like Cole said.

It burns bright in the heart of a lioness.

Grinning, I bite my bottom lip and press my thumb into the vase I'm molding. I like the way Cole sees me. I like the way I feel when I'm with him.

I like a hockey player, Beau's teammate, a guy with a short contract. It's dangerous. It's thrilling.

Right now, it's everything I need.

BEA

I met someone.

CELINE

Stop! Give me deets.

BEA

(Frowning emoji) He's a hockey player.

CELINE

Oh girl…

BEA

Beau's teammate.

CELINE

(Three face palm emojis)

BEA

But I like him.

CELINE

Does Beau know?

BEA

Not yet.

CELINE

This is a recipe for disaster.

BEA

(Shrugging emoji)

CELINE

Okay, who are you? And what have you done
with Bea?

BEA

(Laughing emoji) He's the bright spot in my
new normal.

CELINE

Being back home that bad?

BEA

Not bad…just, the same. Jay's been coming
around.

CELINE

???

BEA

Wants to get back together.

CELINE

This warrants a phone call. FaceTime
tomorrow?

BEA

Early morning? Coffee date?

CELINE

Done. Talk to you then. Keep your head up.
Crown on.

BEA

Always. (Heart emoji)

CELINE CALLS me the following morning while I'm sitting in the window seat, watching the quiet street below.

I grin as soon as I see her face. "You look beautiful!"

She laughs, rolling her eyes. "I'm on set."

"For..."

"New Spielberg film."

"Damn, girl!"

She moves the phone away from her face so I can see more of her glamorous dress. "I'm royalty."

"Yes, you are." I nod enthusiastically. In my mind, Celine Hernandez will always be a queen. Even though she and my brother haven't spoken in years, she's been my one constant female, save for Gran. But talking periods, padded bras, and sex with Gran was a hell of a lot more mortifying.

Celine laughs again before plopping in a chair. "I've got ten minutes before hair and makeup. Spill the tea." I bite the corner of my mouth and she laughs. "You like the hockey player."

"I like the hockey player," I breathe out, confirming it. Then, I tell Celine all about Cole Philips and the way he makes my heart beat faster. I tell her all the reasons why we have no chance, no future, together.

"But you're still going to go for it, aren't you?" she asks when I'm finished.

Rolling my lips together, I nod.

Celine grins. "Then he's worth it, babe."

"You think so?"

A flicker of sadness flares in her dark eyes before she blinks it away. "I know so. The guys you can't stay away from, even when you know you should, are always worth it. Maybe not for forever, but for this moment, you'd regret not giving him a chance."

"I know," I agree. Deep down, I know Celine's right.

I want to get to know Cole Philips. I want him to be worth the risk.

COLE

Why can't a nose be twelve inches long?

I SMILE AS SOON as I see the message. Cole is funny and engaging. More than that, he effortlessly makes me smile.

BEA

Why?

COLE

Because then it'd be a foot.

I snort but my smile widens, big enough that my cheeks ache.

BEA

(Three eyeroll emojis)

COLE

(Smiling emoji) Is it still too presumptuous to ask you for dinner?

I bite my bottom lip, my thumb hovering over the keypad.

BEA

No...

My phone rings a moment later.

I answer. "My response warrants a phone call?"

Cole's deep, measured voice replies, "Absolutely. After that joke, I didn't want to leave anything to chance."

I chuckle and sink to the edge of my bed, clasping a pillow to my chest.

Cole clears his throat, the teasing lilt of his tone gone when he asks, "Would you have dinner with me, Bea?"

"Yes," I breathe out, almost breathless. Is this what it feels like when the man you desire asks you out?

With Jay, it was always a given that we would pass our weekends together, sometimes with friends, sometimes without. In art school, I dated. But it almost always happened by chance, a guy and I pairing off together at the end of a long, alcohol-infused night, or due to a group project assigned in class that turned into grabbing dinner.

"Yeah?" I hear the smile in Cole's voice. "I'd like to cook for you then."

"You cook?" I can't hide the surprise in my tone and Cole laughs.

"Not particularly well but I'm going to pull out all the stops."

At his candid response, I giggle. "Okay. I'd like that too."

"How's Thursday night? We have a game on Friday."

"Thursday is perfect. I'll be at your game; I'm working."

"Oh, right. Then you have to come for drinks afterwards," Cole says. "The team usually ends up at Corks."

I shake my head. Corks has been around a long time. "The Bolts were successful in wrangling control of Corks from the Coyotes?"

Cole chuckles. "Nah, it's more of a shared custody agreement. Both teams stick to our own sides."

"I can see that," I admit. "Okay, well, we'll see how Thursday dinner goes before I commit to Friday drinks."

"Ouch." Cole fake whimpers. "You think I can't impress you, Bea?"

I bite the corner of my mouth. I'm already impressed. I'm already excited and giddy and desperate for Thursday night to arrive. But I manage to keep my cool when I respond. "Time will tell, Cole."

"Challenge accepted. I'll pick you up at—"

"It's okay. Send me your address and I'll come by."

"You sure?"

"Absolutely."

"Okay. I'll text you. Does 6 PM work?"

"That's perfect. I'll bring dessert."

"Please not cupcakes."

I laugh, knowing just how many Primrose cupcakes Cole Philips has consumed in the past month. I love that he continued to buy and eat them just to talk to me. I love that Cole thinks enough of me to continue to seek me out. "Not cupcakes," I promise.

"Okay. See you soon, Bea."

"Thursday," I confirm.

When I hang up, I squee and perform a little dance around my bedroom. I can't dance for shit so it's awkward and mortifying, but I don't care. I have a date with Cole Philips.

Picking up my phone, I text Celine.

BEA

I have a date.

CELINE

Hockey player?

BEA

He's cooking us dinner.

CELINE

Damn, girl. He LIKES you.

BEA

I hope so.

CELINE

You tell Beau?

BEA

Not yet...

CELINE

Don't wait too long.

BEA

Yeah...

I toss my phone down. I'll tell Beau later, when I'm not caught up in my excitement.

When I'm not frantically flipping through the hangers in my closet wondering what the hell I'm supposed to wear for a dinner date with Cole freaking Philips!

SIX

COLE

"YOU GOTTA GO BIG," Jamie says, her tone decisive.

"How big?" I muse, clicking on another online recipe. Nope, I definitely can't pull off a mango mahi-mahi ceviche.

"Big."

I roll my eyes. "Like, pulled pork big or—"

"You don't have a smoker there, do you?"

"No."

"Keep thinking."

"I can order takeout, you know?"

Jamie sighs. "Cole, you invited her over and offered to make her dinner. You have to actually *make* her dinner."

"I got it!" I snap. "Beef Wellington."

"You're going to make Beef Wellington?" Now, Jamie sounds skeptical.

"You said big!"

She laughs. "I know, but—"

"You don't think I can handle it?"

"Not even a little," my cousin replies with blatant honesty.

I grin, not put off in the least. "May I remind you who won the family pie competition?"

Jamie giggles. "It was pie eating, not pie making, Cole Philips."

I snort. "I can handle it, Jaim. Trust me."

"I do. I…I just want this to go well for you."

I soften toward my cousin. In every way that matters, she's like my sister. "I do too. I'm trying to impress her."

"You play in the NHL; I'm sure she's already impressed."

"Nope." I shake my head, even though Jamie can't see me. Popping in my EarPods, I continue, "Her brother is our goalie."

Silence descends on the conversation for a handful of moments. Then, laughter. Sputtering laughter. Followed by a groan. "You're dating your teammate's sister?"

More choked laughter. Then, a wheeze.

Jesus. "Why are you having the reaction you're having?"

"I want this to work for you, Cole!" She's exasperated now.

I frown. "Why wouldn't it?"

"Your teammate's sister? That's an unnecessary complication. And I know you. You don't date often, but whenever you have a relationship, even a friendship, you get too invested. You have high expectations."

I bite my lip. Jamie's right. I do have high expectations. I saw firsthand what a relationship looks like when one partner expects jack shit from the other and it's a trainwreck I don't want to live out again. "I like Bea."

"I know. And I think it's time for you to get out there and try, for real, with a woman you like."

Sighing, I pull out a chair and sit down at my kitchen table. I love my cousin but sometimes, I hate the circles we talk around to arrive at the point. What is the damn point? "And…?"

"Don't try so hard that you mess it up. Beef Wellington is a serious commitment."

"I can handle it."

Jamie sighs. "Fine. But if it burns, have a backup plan."

"Don't need one," I verbally shoot her idea down but make a mental note of it. It's not an awful suggestion, not that I'd tell her.

"I'm happy for you, Cole," Jamie gentles her tone. "I just want you to be happy."

"I know. I appreciate it."

"You've held back for a long time. If you're willing to try —really try—with your teammate's little sister, then she must be special."

"She is."

Another sigh. "So, Beef Wellington?"

I snort. "Yeah, Jaim. Got any tips?"

"A few." My cousin launches into a speech involving candlesticks and linen napkins. Types of pairing wines and best desserts. When she pauses to suck in an inhale, I interject.

"How long have you been saving this speech?"

Jamie laughs. "I've been waiting years for you to meet a woman you want to impress."

I smile, liking that it's Bea. "Me too."

"I'm proud of you, Cole. Now, make sure you have a fresh haircut and dress nice for the occasion. It isn't every day you attempt Beef Wellington."

I chuckle, agreeing. "Are you saying if I look good, she may overlook a burned dinner?"

"Anything that helps…"

I laugh again but file that tidbit away too. I want to improve my chances with Bea. Enough to cut my hair and spend an entire night googling Beef Wellington and side dish recipes.

I FUCKED this up big time.

Instead of taking an assist, I tried for a damn breakaway.

I am not someone who owns a food processor. At least, I wasn't until this morning. I've never worked with puff pastry before. Nor have I ever used a brush to gently add an egg wash to pastry. My countertop ran out of room for the plastic wrap needed to wrap the beef together and I tried to use dental floss as a substitute for twine.

It didn't work.

Every surface space in my kitchen is currently occupied. Shit, I'm sweating. The fingerling potatoes are taking longer to roast than I thought. The Beef Wellington is both burned and soggy—what the actual fuck? And my kitchen looks like a science experiment gone very, very wrong.

What was I thinking?

I'm not cut out for serious. I'm not a guy who can handle a spatula with the ease I control a hockey stick. I am not the guy who cooks a fancy dinner for a woman.

Frantically, I rush around the kitchen, my arms extended, palms spread wide, as if I can somehow pull it all together before my lovely date arrives.

But it's hopeless. One, I don't know where the fuck to begin. Two, I spent hours—hours, plural—waiting in line for the most amazing buttermilk pie. Even though Bea is bringing dessert, I couldn't resist. It's a southern staple and the bakery, Annabelle's, always has a line out the door. While waiting, I grossly underestimated how much time I needed to create the Beef Wellington masterpiece.

On what planet did I think I was capable of whipping this together? I eat grilled chicken and kale salad or salmon and a baked potato every night for dinner. My meal plan is rock solid and I rarely, if ever, deviate. I'm almost always in train- ing, tracking my nutrition, logging my miles, recording my weight training sessions.

And, if I'm being honest, my month of daily cupcake

consumption derailed my progress. Now I need to recommit, big time, if I want to play my best on the ice. Tonight with Bea is my last hurrah before I tighten the reins and get my training back on track.

I'm supposed to enjoy this evening, this dinner, just *being* with the woman I like. Instead, I'm about to have a heart attack.

Dread fills my stomach, weighing it down like a rock, as I take in the disaster of my kitchen. The dining table is set for dinner, complete with wine glasses and candlesticks. But there's nothing to serve.

I have nothing to feed Bea!

A loud beep cuts through my chaotic thoughts. "Fuck!" I swear loudly as the smoke detector sounds. Rushing to find a dish towel, I come up empty-handed. I race to the bathroom, grab the hand towel off the sink, and begin to wave it back and forth below the smoke detector, silently praying for the beeping to cease.

Sweat beads along my hairline and the back of my neck prickles with worry. What the hell is my backup plan? Didn't Jamie tell me to have a backup?

I jump up and down a few times, waving the towel, until finally—finally!—the loud wail turns off.

"Jesus," I breathe out, sagging against the wall.

I close my eyes, momentarily shutting out the mess, my failed meal, the disappointment I feel for letting down Bea. There's no way she's going to want to explore things between us when I've screwed this dinner, this date, up so badly. What woman would?

I exhale slowly. An endless loop of challenges I've faced— of people who have doubted me—flows through my mind.

You're never going to cut it.

You don't have what it takes, Cole.

With your upbringing? Good luck.

You'll be dead by thirty, just like your folks.

You're never going to make it. Never going to have it.
Never. Never. Never.

My eyes snap open. I've been battling negativity my entire life. With my childhood—a hotbed of drugs and abuse—I never should have made it as far as I have. No one, save for my coaches, Uncle Kirk, and Jamie, ever bet on me. Except me. I always bet on myself, and that belief is why I've overcome so many hurdles.

Am I really going to back down now, lose to Beef fucking Wellington?

Looking at my watch, I realize I have an hour. One hour to turn this shit around. To make an impression. To own my mistake and turn it into an unforgettable moment that makes Bea laugh. That makes her like me back.

Resolve settles over me and I spring into action. Grabbing a black garbage bag, I throw out my failed attempt at dinner. I toss everything I can in the dishwasher and pile everything else in the sink. Forty minutes.

Pulling open my refrigerator, I take quick stock of what I have on hand. Various combinations of food—grilled chicken and potatoes, peanut butter and jelly sandwiches, could I make crepes? Nope, out of peanut butter and bananas—runs through my mind. And then—pizza English muffins!

Jamie and I used to make them all the time as snacks/dinner when we were tweens. With Uncle Kirk working two, sometimes three, jobs, we were left on our own for most dinners.

For the most part, we ate sandwiches. As we got older, I'd scramble some eggs and Jaim would make pancakes and we'd have breakfast supper. But our staple, the thing we did on Friday nights and when either of us had a shitty day, whether from school, hockey, or a member of the opposite sex, we made pizza on English muffins.

Jaime was right; I needed a backup.

Laughing to myself, I pull out the necessary ingredients

and whip up what I can. When I have seven minutes left, I beeline to my bedroom to change.

Jeans, a polo, and a pair of sneakers. I style my hair, brush my teeth, and am spraying on cologne when the doorbell rings.

She's here!

I take a calming breath and stare at myself in the mirror.

"Prove them wrong," I mutter to my reflection, the words I've said like a mantra my entire life. *Prove them wrong.*

Then, I waltz toward the front door and pull it open.

Bea looks like a deer caught in headlights, her frame rounding in on itself like she's unsure if she's in the right place. Immediately, my tension eases and my want to put her at ease rises to the surface.

I smile at her and she relaxes, giving me a smile back. Her curls are pulled away from her face, a few errant corkscrews framing her face and brushing against the nape of her neck. She's wearing makeup, her eyes a soft grey, her mouth a luscious pout.

She rocks the hell out of a tight pair of jeans and a simple, hunter-green sweater. Her cowgirl boots punch up her outfit and make me smile.

"You look beautiful," I say.

She blushes. My smile widens.

"I, I'm nervous," she admits, standing straighter. She presses a pastry box into my hands. "They're cookies."

At her confession, every panicked thought I had about messing up dinner evaporates. She's nervous? About this? With me?

I make an exaggerated bow and sweep my arm holding the cookie box toward the living room.

"Welcome, my lady. I'm so glad you could join me for dinner." I wink. "Thank you for the cookies."

Bea giggles but she crosses the threshold, her nose

scrunching up as she breathes in burnt beef and pastry. Her face swings to mine, eyes questioning.

"This evening, I've created an exquisite meal. There's a long, and important, history behind this particular dish. It's one of the most popular, most sought-after, plates in the world. It is truly my honor to serve it to you this evening." I move toward the kitchen with Bea following close behind me.

When I glance at her over my shoulder, her eyes are wide, her expression unreadable.

I snicker as I pull open the oven door and give her another one of my exaggerated bows. "May I present, English muffin pizzas! They're even personalized."

Bea's face is frozen in shock as she comes to a complete stop. Her eyes swing from the oven rack to my face and back again.

I bite the inside of my cheek. "I burned the Beef Wellington."

At my confession, Bea tips her head back and laughs. It's a carefree, spontaneous sound, like when a child erupts with giggles. Her curls shake, her neck is long and graceful, and her eyes dance with mirth when they meet mine.

Her expression is so candid, she's so damn beautiful, that I wish she'd keep laughing at me.

Bea wipes the corner of her eye and shakes her head. "Oh, Cole, I'm so glad I met you," she admits.

That, right there, makes my Beef Wellington failure worth it. "Then, I'll try to butcher more dinners."

Her laughter starts back up as she reaches for my arm. She squeezes my shoulder and I try not to flex my bicep because I'm not River Patton. "Just, please, always be yourself."

"Only if you promise to be yourself too."

Her eyes sober as they latch onto mine. For a long moment, we stare at each other, our eyes saying much more than our words.

I'm nervous. I don't do this. I messed it up. I like you.

Bea nods. "Deal."

I gesture toward the dining table. "Want a glass of wine? I swear, that's supposed to be good."

She grins and moves toward the dining table. Over her shoulder, she gives me an innocent look that heats my blood like a smolder. "Pizza's my favorite."

"Mine too."

SEVEN
BEA

COLE WENT ALL OUT for this dinner date. His apartment is small but clean. The dining table is covered in a navy-blue tablecloth. Two candlesticks, heavy and ornate, sit in the center of the table. They look like something he inherited from his gran or purchased at a yard sale. The ivory candles in them are fresh and knowing that he probably never used them before—that he may have bought them for tonight, for me—fills me with a lightness.

A flutter of excitement zips through my body.

I take in the simple place settings. The gleaming wine glasses. It's thoughtful and sweet.

For all the years Jay and I dated, he never cooked for me. Sure, he did other things, but they existed in the realm of "a man's work," that his father instilled in him. Cooking is for the women. So is cleaning and laundry and raising the children.

Jay would change the oil in my car and hang shelves in my bedroom.

If he had ventured into cooking dinner and burnt the meal, he'd be furious. Probably yelling that the whole thing is my fault—since I should have been the one cooking in the first place.

Not Cole. No, Cole owned his mistake, laughing it off with a sheepish shrug and an adorable grin.

He turned what could have been a disastrous date into one of the best I've ever experienced. All because of his humor, his willingness to laugh at himself, his desire to enjoy this moment with me more than uphold an expectation.

"My lady." Cole enters the dining room. He brings the delicious scent of pizza and basil with him.

I turn away from the window and when I meet his gaze, time stops. Everything stops. Cole's blue eyes flash. Amusement colors their bottomless depths but underneath, a glimmer of seriousness shines. He feels it too.

The tug between us; the natural pull. We connect in a way that's as exhilarating as it is terrifying. Partly because it's new but mostly, I think, because it's *new* for us.

"Thank you, kind sir," I play along, sitting down at the table.

Cole presents the English muffin pizzas, placing the tray in the center of the table. He pours us each a glass of wine and takes the seat across from mine.

Lifting his glass in the air, he chuckles. "To pizza and lionesses."

I snort, the sound as natural as it is unattractive. Clinking my glass against Cole's, I take a deep sip. An appreciative groan falls from my mouth. "This is delicious."

"Glad I got one thing right." He places two slices of English muffin pizzas on my plate.

"More than one," I reassure him, taking a bite and moaning again.

"Thanks for being a good sport about this." He takes a bite of his pizza.

"Are you kidding? This is delicious."

Cole shakes his head. "I'm just glad you're not running for

the door." At the vulnerability rounding out his tone, I soften more.

"Not a chance, Cole Philips. You're a lot more interesting than just a hockey player."

He laughs, his eyes crinkling in the corners. "Because I can't cook?"

"Because of your outlook. You're always calm, always in control of your emotions. When things don't go the way you want, you pivot."

He tilts his head, studying me. "Our team captain—"

"Devon Hardt." I lift an eyebrow.

"Yes, Devon. He's been coaching me, pushing me, to be more assertive."

"Standing up for yourself is never a bad thing. It's something I'm working on too."

"Really?"

I nod. "I hate letting people down."

"I hate confrontation. Anything that has the chance of becoming violent—hell, even awkward—I want nothing to do with it," he admits it like a confession. But then, his eyes sharpen on mine. "Who could you possibly let down?"

I shrug, not knowing how much to confide in Cole. It's strange, because already, I trust him. But he also knows, is teammates, with Beau. "My brothers sacrificed a lot for me to have as much of a normal childhood as possible."

He dips his head in understanding. "I'm sorry about your parents, Bea. Mine passed too."

I straighten in my chair, my pizza forgotten. "Both of them?"

Cole nods, wiping a napkin over his mouth. "Drug overdose. They were junkies."

A vice grips my heart, squeezing it painfully. I know what it's like to lose parents, to wake up without the nucleus of the family holding it all together. I've always known that my parents would have moved mountains to not die in that helicopter crash. Their deaths were the results of a tragic, unthinkable accident.

But Cole's parents…drug addicts. That type of grief leaves you with a different kind of loss. "I had no idea," I murmur. "I don't even know what to say. That must have been devastating."

He swirls the wine in his glass, staring at the bold red color, before taking a sip. "This is pretty heavy for a first date—"

"We don't have to talk about it."

He shakes his head. "I don't mind telling you. It's strange, because I never tell people about my family, but with you, Bea…I don't want there to be secrets."

"Me neither," I say, meaning it. It's been a long time since I've gotten to know a man, but I want to know everything about Cole. How did he survive his parents' loss? Who did he live with? Does he carry around the same survivor's guilt I sometimes struggle with?

Does he have people he'd do anything to not disappoint?

"My parents were terrible people. Maybe not always, but from what I remember…they weren't really fit to be parents. Hockey was my out and I took it. I was in a tournament a few states away when they OD'ed. And as awful as it fucking is…" He trails off, offering me an embarrassed smile. "Their deaths confused the hell out of me. I was both devastated and relieved."

My heart breaks as I think of him as a little boy, constantly surrounded by chaos and uncertainty. Living in an unstable environment with questions and concerns. Cole's upbringing much have been intense and difficult, confusing and hurtful.

"Don't feel sorry for me," he murmurs, his eyes losing some of their warmth. "I turned out all right."

"You turned out incredible," I state. "I hardly know you and yet, I like being with you. I like the way I feel around you, more than most of the people I've known my entire life."

The tension in his shoulders subsides and he relaxes. "I've worked really hard to break the cycle. To not become my parents. To prove everyone who thought I'd amount to nothing—so pretty much everyone from my childhood—wrong."

"Is that why you don't like confrontation?"

He nods slowly, his eyes holding mine. "I avoid it at all costs."

I take a sip of wine and then, spill one of my own secrets. "I didn't want to move back."

Cole frowns. "To take care of Gran?"

Guilt multiplies in my stomach. "I want to take care of Gran. Not because of an expectation but because I really do love her, and she sacrificed so much for my brothers and me. But, if Gran wasn't ill, I wouldn't have come back home."

"Where would you go?" Curiosity colors Cole's voice and he leans back in his chair.

"New York. L.A. Maybe Europe? Anywhere but here."

"You feel like you're settling?" He hits the nail on the head.

"Sometimes, yes. But I don't *want* to feel that way."

"Does Beau know?"

I bite the bottom of my lip, a lick of panic swiping at my belly.

"I'd never say anything," Cole rushes out. "He cares about you. A lot."

"I love my brother," I say. "He sacrificed the most for me. Enlisting in the military paid my way for art school. It's been tough for him, readjusting to civilian life. Hockey, the chance with the Bolts, means everything to him." I halt, not wanting to share too much of Beau's personal life. As much as I want to confide in Cole, I can't do it at the expense of Beau. Not when so much of his career, his future, is tied up with the Thunderbolts. "It's my turn to take care of Gran. It's my turn to step up for my brothers, the way they always have for me."

Cole watches me for a long moment before nodding slowly. "I understand that. I feel the same way about helping my family." Surprise must bloom in my expression because Cole adds, "My uncle Kirk and cousin Jamie took me in after my parents passed. Even before that, Uncle Kirk was working two jobs and paying my way for hockey. He raised me as his son, provided for me more than my father ever did. Jamie is like my sister. We were raised together and always have each other's backs. Even now, my uncle works, even though he should have retired a few years back. He says it's to keep busy and stick to a routine, but I think he's intent on providing Jamie with a down payment for a first home in the future. He's a provider by nature, but it's cost him quality of life."

"And you want to help?"

"I'd do anything for him. For both of them. As soon as I signed with the Bolts, I paid off my uncle's mortgage and Jamie's student loans. I thought that would alleviate some financial pressure and convince Uncle Kirk to retire."

His loyalty to his family is one I understand well. I live it. "We're more alike than different, you know?"

"I know. I was drawn to you the moment I saw you, little lioness. Underneath that uncertainty, you've got strength, pride, an edge I hope you let loose one day."

I roll my lips together, smiling to lighten the conversation. "You think you can handle my ferocity, Cole?"

He chuckles. "I hope you let me witness it, Bea. I hope you give me the chance I'm after."

I've never had a man speak to me so candidly before. Cole shows his cards, laying them all out on the table. Any other guy would think it's too early. That we don't know each other enough. Maybe they'd be right, but I like that Cole trusts his instincts. I like that he knows what he wants and isn't afraid to admit it. To put himself out there, rejection be damned.

"What chance is that?" I ask, wanting the confirmation.

He grins, not at all put off by my forwardness. "You. I want a chance with you, Bea. I want to tell Beau that I'm dating you, that we're getting to know each other. There's no rush, but I don't want to hide this." He gestures between us.

My heart nearly leaps out of my chest. "I want that too," I admit. "But, please, let me tell Beau."

He frowns. "I don't want him to think I'm going behind his back."

"He won't," I assure him. "I know my brother; I need to break this news to him."

Cole laughs and tops up our wine glasses. Holding his up to me, he asks, "So, does this mean you'll come to Corks tomorrow night?"

"I'll be there," I promise, clinking his wine glass and taking a long sip. "I can't wait to celebrate your win."

"Now you're just inflating my ego."

"You don't have an ego, Cole Philips," I tell him truthfully. "It's one of the things I like most about you."

EIGHT
COLE

"NO WAY!" Bea exclaims as I return to the dining table, a buttermilk pie in one hand, the cookies she brought in the other. "You must have waited hours for Annabelle's."

I shrug, feigning casual, even though the long wait time at the bakery meant cutting my workout short. Will I make up the missed reps tonight? Will my training slip now that I've missed part of a workout? Can I even have a slice of pie after all the Primrose cupcakes I consumed last month? I clear my throat. "It wasn't too bad."

I can tell from Bea's expression that she doesn't buy it. Instead of calling me out, her smile widens. "I love Annabelle's pies."

"They are a massive draw of living in Tennessee," I agree. "I'll be right back with coffee." As I hurry to retrieve our coffee mugs, Bea slices and serves the pie.

Sitting across from her, pie and candlesticks between us, I realize how much I've grown up. How much I've learned to let people into my life. For years, it's been hockey over everything. In the past, I never would have shortened a workout to buy a pie.

I'm proud of myself for enjoying this evening with Bea.

Right now, I'm trying to have both—a professional and personal life—and I think I'm pulling it off okay.

"Do you like living here?" Bea asks, taking a sip of coffee.

I nod. "I like anywhere that allows me to play hockey for a living. But, yes, the Bolts are a great group of guys. I'm lucky to be on the team."

"Not luck. You worked for it."

"Yeah," I agree. "But the work doesn't go away. If anything, it gets more intense."

"Is it worth it?" Her fork hovers over her plate, her eyes pinned on mine.

"I think so," I admit. "To live your passion as a career? What could be more worth it than that?"

Bea gives me a little smile and a nod. Then, she uses the edge of her fork to cut a bite of pie and places it in her mouth. Her eyes close and the most appreciative, most uninhibited sound, rings out.

I can't tear my eyes away from watching her enjoy buttermilk pie. My jeans feel too tight. My shirt, restrictive. Bea Turner is one of the most innocent, sweet, genuine women I've ever met.

But behind her rounded shoulders and creamy skin is a strong, fierce, gorgeous woman desperate to be seen. And I see her.

I want to see all of her.

"Do you want to get out of here after coffee and pie?" I ask, surprising myself as the thought pops into my mind.

Any other guy I know—River Patton comes to mind— would try to get Bea to stay. He'd want to relax with some drinks, mess around a little, get a girl in his bed for sunrise.

Bea quirks an eyebrow, a mischievous smirk curling half of her mouth. "What are you thinking?"

"You been to the Art Attic yet?"

Confusion ripples over Bea's face and she shakes her head.

"Brawler—you know Axel Daire?"

Bea nods.

"He took his girl Maisy there a few months ago for a wine and paint night. Apparently, it's a new place, combining art classes with a little bistro and bar."

"Here? In our tiny town?" Bea sounds skeptical. I understand her surprise. Only forty minutes outside of Knoxville, this town has managed to stay off the radar and maintain a quiet, country lane feel.

But as the city expands outward, coupled with the University of Tennessee campus, more small businesses and storefronts are popping up. The Art Attic, a space for creatives and amateurs alike, is one of those spots. I glance at my watch. It's nearly eight but since the Art Attic draws a lot of students, it keeps late hours.

"You want to check it out?" I ask. By the curiosity shading Bea's eyes, she's definitely intrigued. I want her to see the space and I want to experience it with her. That joy, that excitement, that need, that fills your veins when you're passionate about something.

Bea stares at me, her expression unreadable. An intensity shimmers around her, like an aura. "You'll take me?"

"I *want* to take you."

"Then, yes. Let's go."

I take a small bite of the pie, my shortened workout shadowing the back of my mind. Bea finishes her coffee. We stand up and she reaches for our dirty plates, stacking them. I touch her wrist. "Leave them."

"What?" Her eyebrows bend as if she misheard me.

I shake my head. "You want to see the Art Attic or clean my kitchen?"

"But when you get back tonight—"

"I'll wash the dishes," I assure her. "Come on." I shrug into a zip up and grab my keys, wallet, and phone off the kitchen counter.

Bea settles the strap of her purse across her chest. An excited, almost childish gleam brightens her eyes. "You sure about this, Cole?"

"Surer than anything else," I toss out, locking the door behind us.

As we walk down my driveway, a breeze kicks up and Bea shivers. I wrap an arm around her shoulders. "You want a hoodie?" Even though she's wearing a sweater, the material is thin, and tonight is cooler than usual.

She looks up at me, her grey eyes dark, her lips pursed. I stop walking. Bea stills beside me, a small gasp falling from her lips.

"Bea," I whisper, "are you cold?"

She shakes her head. The movement is slow. Her gaze doesn't waver from mine. Around us, the sky darkens and the stars blink. The wind ripples over us, a cool blast that brushes Bea's hair back from her face. She turns into me and my other arm lifts, my hand palming her hip.

My heart is thrumming so loudly, it pounds in my eardrums. My fingers curl into her softness, soaking up the heat of her skin through her thin sweater. God, she's gorgeous. Her grey eyes are slate, shadowed in sadness, shimmering with an edge of hope. She tips her head back farther, giving me her expressions, the want and desire she's too nervous to act on.

I work a swallow, my throat clogged with sand. Do I make a move? If I kiss her, will it change things? Will it cross the line of casually getting to know each other into something more serious?

I don't do anything by halves. I'm always all in or all out. For years, hockey has been my everything. *Prove them all wrong.* Why would my relationship with a woman be anything less than all I'm capable of giving?

Bea's lips part, soft and inviting.

Desire flares to life in my limbs, sweeping my body with

heat I've only felt in the middle of sex. Never over the anticipation of a simple kiss. Never this quickly and fervently.

"Bea," I murmur her name. *Tell me what you want. Grant me the permission to take your mouth and devour it.*

As if she hears my silent plea, her chin lifts, her eyes widen, and my mouth lands on hers. I grip Bea, pulling her against my chest, as my arms encircle her frame. Her hands are trapped between us, palms flat on my chest. But she pushes up onto her toes and deepens our kiss.

Our lips brush, gentle and sweet. But when Bea dips her tongue into my mouth, everything escalates. I slant my mouth over hers and kiss her with years of pent-up desire, with years of wanting to find a woman as breathtakingly beautiful as her.

She makes a little sound in the back of her throat, a tiny mewl, like a kitten lapping at milk. Satisfied yet greedy for more. The sound clangs in my head, both a warning and an encouragement.

I want to devour Bea. I want to haul her back inside my house and lay her out in my bed. I want to see her auburn ringlets on my pillowcase and breathe in the scent of her skin —vanilla and lavender.

But I also want her to know how much I respect her. How much I value her and this thing brewing between us. That I don't do things like this with random women. I play hockey and I go home. I train and I hang with my team.

For me, women have always been a beautiful distraction. With Bea, I want more.

Forcing myself to break our connection, I step back. I grip her waist, holding her until she meets my gaze. Desire clouds her eyes, a flicker of vulnerability flaring from their depths.

"I don't want to rush this with you, Bea," I blurt out the truth. "I want this to mean something."

"It does."

"Good." I grin. "Then let's give it the time it deserves."

A surprised chuckle falls from her mouth. "I've never been given the letdown so sweetly before."

I wrap my arm around her shoulder and steer her toward my car. "It's not a letdown, lioness. It's a pledge."

"A pledge?"

I open the passenger door. Before she can slip inside, I grip her hand and place it flat against my heart. "I promise to be a man worthy of your attention. Affection. Of whatever the hell you give me, I'll keep it safe, Bea."

"You're messing this up, big-time, for any other guy I ever date." She bites her bottom lip. Her tone is amused but I see the seriousness in her expression, I note the hint of vulnerability in her eyes.

I chuckle to lighten the mood, kiss the tip of her fingers, and release her.

As I round the car, I realize how much Bea doesn't know about me. In all fairness, how could she? We're just getting to know each other. And it's not the norm for a hockey player, for a professional athlete, to only play for keeps.

But if I have my way, there won't be any other men dating Bea. Because I'll be enough. I'll be her last first everything. And neither of us will have any regrets.

I slide behind the wheel of my car and glance over at Bea. She's buckled in, her body humming with the same excitement, the same hope, that sparks in mine.

Our drive to the Art Attic is comfortable. A Sam Hunt song plays quietly in the background. We're both lost in our thoughts. I'm consumed by the kiss we shared and the promise of a night that isn't over yet. I hope she is too.

When we enter the Art Attic, a striking woman greets us. "Welcome to the Art Attic. I'm Mel."

"Bea." Bea sticks out a hand. "I had no idea this even opened." A thread of awe weaves through her words, her eyes drinking in the space. "This is incredible."

"Cole." I wave in introduction.

Mel smiles. "Let me show you around. Then, you can tell me what you're interested in creating tonight. And, of course, if you're hungry."

Bea falls into step with Mel. Mel points out different workspaces and fills Bea in on the different classes and artistic mediums utilized by the teachers here.

"Bea Turner?" Mel says after a beat. "I saw your showcase in Nashville last year."

Bea comes to a complete halt, her cheeks burning bright red. She worries her bottom lip between her teeth.

"It was incredible," Mel gushes, unaware just how nervous Bea is for her approval. "You are so talented, and I loved your collection of vases."

Bea's eyes swim with emotion and I step behind her, placing a hand in the center of her back to steady her.

Mel tips her head. "Have you considered teaching? We could use someone with your expertise with some of the pottery classes, especially for our advanced students."

Bea's fingers press against her chest, as if confirming that Mel is speaking to her. "Seriously?"

"Seriously," Mel says, holding up a finger. "Let me give you my card. I'd love to sit down this week and discuss your availability, if you're interested?"

"I'm interested."

Mel grins. "I'll be right back."

As Mel moves back to the front desk for a card, Bea turns into me. Wonder washes over her expression. "Can you believe that? I could work here, work with clay, and be…in an art world. Every day, Cole. I could do this every day."

At the unbridled happiness, the pride, in her tone, I dip my head and brush a kiss to her lips. I can't help myself. I love seeing my lioness embrace her purpose. Revel in it. "They'd be lucky to have you."

Mel returns and settles us into a workspace. "What are you going to sculpt?"

Bea smirks. "Want to start with a little vase? For a succulent?"

I laugh and stretch out my palms, wiggling my fingers. "I'm ready, babe. Teach me."

Mel leaves us to it and after a quick introduction, Bea places her hands over mine and teaches me how to shape clay before we move toward a spinning wheel. "You ready?"

I fall into the softness of her grey eyes. Am I ready for everything Bea Turner is gifting me?

"Let's do it."

NINE

BEA

"HEY!" I shout out my open bedroom door as Beau moves down the hallway like a herd of elephants.

He pops his head into my bedroom. "You okay?"

"Yeah." I frown. "Are you?"

He sighs, tapping the butt of his fist against the doorjamb. Tension coils in his neck and I feel the frustration radiating off him. "Can't find this new blocking glove. I thought I left it at The Honeycomb but..." He trails off, shaking his head. "Forget it. You coming to the game tonight?"

I shift my legs off my bed and stand, walking toward Beau. I want to talk to him; I want to tell him about Cole, the way I promised. "I'm working the game tonight," I remind him.

A small smile tips his mouth upward. "That's right. How's it working out at Primrose? Sorry, things have been so busy, we haven't caught up in a minute."

"Primrose is good. And you're right. Do you have a minute? There's something I want to talk to you about."

A frown mars Beau's expression. He opens his mouth and his phone rings. Swearing, he pulls it out of his back pocket.

Beau's eyebrows knit together at the name of the caller. He shakes the phone at me. "I gotta take this, Bea. You okay?"

"Yeah, I'm fine."

He answers the call. "Hey, man. Give me one minute, yeah?" He nods at me to continue, his eyes serious, his hand clenched around his cell phone.

Does he expect me to pour out my soul in this moment? With a stranger listening in through his phone? A bead of frustration sits on the tip of my tongue, but I swallow it back. Beau is clearly stressed—whether about tonight's game, or something else, I have no clue—but I don't want to burden my brother before he takes the ice.

"I'm fine," I repeat. "Just, when you have some time, can we talk?"

Guilt radiates off Beau and I instantly feel worse. "Of course, Bea. After the game, yeah?"

I nod, forcing a smile to put him at ease. "Sure. Good luck tonight."

"Thanks," he says, shifting the phone closer to his ear. "What's good, man?"

I watch Beau walk down the hallway and down the steps. I hear the screen door fling open, smacking against the house.

Sighing, I sit down on my bed and check my phone. I have a few hours before I need to be at The Honeycomb. I smile at Celine's text.

CELINE

Good night kiss?

BEA

Better...

CELINE

SHUT UP! Did y'all (eggplant emoji + okay hand emoji)?

Laughter rolls up my throat and explodes into the silence

of the house. Holy shit! I clutch my pillow to my chest, laughing so hard at Celine's reaction. Somehow, even though Gran swears her hearing is going, she's disturbed by my raucous laughter. A moment later, the thump of her broom handle hitting the ceiling below me rings out. It makes me laugh harder.

BEA

I'm dead. Laughing so hard, Gran is hitting the ceiling with her broom.

CELINE

Oh God! Haha! I miss Gran!

BEA

You're coming to her birthday bash in April... right???

Every year, Gran has a big blowout for her birthday. This year, she's turning ninety, and friends and family around the country are flying in to surprise her. This year's theme is a Hawaiian Luau.

BEA

Even Blake and Brody are flying in.

CELINE

And Beau will be there.

I sigh when she points out the obvious. Of course Beau will be here now that he's back from serving in the Marines. Celine and Beau haven't seen each other since Beau enlisted, but that doesn't mean they can avoid each other forever.

Before I tap out a reply, she messages again.

CELINE

Of course I'll be there. I won't ever miss
Gran's celebration. It's just weird, knowing
Beau and I will see each other, after all these
years.

BEA

True. But it has to happen eventually.

CELINE

I know. Now, tell me about the good night
kiss...(three fire emojis)

I grin, pressing my fingers against my lips as I recall the
smoking hot kiss Cole gave me in his driveway. And then, the
other one he left me with at the end of Gran's driveway. After
I retrieved my car from his house, he insisted on following me
home since it was so late.

Secretly, I love how thoughtful he is. Also secretly, I think
he only did it to kiss me again. But who am I to complain?

BEA

It was the hottest good night kiss of my life.

CELINE

Get it, B! When do you see him again?

BEA

Tonight. Drinks after the game.

CELINE

Team going?

BEA

Yes...

CELINE

Tell your brother! He hates being caught off
guard.

BEA

Trying to...keeps blowing me off.

CELINE

He loves you, B. He just gets lost in his head sometimes.

BEA

I know. I'll keep you posted.

CELINE

Big kiss. See you next month.

BEA

Can't wait (heart emoji)

Tossing down my phone, I lay back on my bed and close my eyes. Even after all these years, and all the hurt between them, Celine won't utter a bad word, a negative comment, even when it's the truth, about Beau. Deep down, she still cares. And by his total avoidance of anything that has to do with her, even her name, I know he does too.

Clearly, April's birthday bash is going to be a shitshow. But, with all my brothers home, that's a given.

Wait. I sit up, my eyes flying open. Will Cole want to come? Should he come? I mean, if we're dating, I'd invite my boyfriend to Gran's party, wouldn't I?

Will Cole be my boyfriend? Are we going to go the traditional, labels and titles, route? He does seem like a traditional guy...

But not traditional the same way Jay is. Jay is more gender-role, man of the house, what I say goes, traditional. Cole seems more caring and nurturing, like he wants to protect and respect me more than anything else.

Sigh. I settle back against my pillows. Everything with Cole moved at warp speed and yet, not. Because the time we spend together, we're talking. We're sharing and confiding and giving pieces of ourselves to each other for safekeeping.

There's a trust between us that's never developed between me and a member of the opposite sex, not counting my brothers, so quickly before. When I'm with Cole, I'm not worried about a potential fallout. I'm not scared something I say will be used against me or that I'll always be held to those words, for the rest of my life, the way I was with Jay. I'm free to be who I am in the moment, and he respects me for it.

I like the woman I'm becoming. I worked hard to sculpt her into existence during my time in Nashville. I found pieces of her through pottery, but the more significant parts, I discovered through my conversations, my exposure, to others. Students, artists, creatives, entrepreneurs.

In Nashville, I felt like I was blossoming into my truest self. When I returned home, back to my childhood bedroom, Beau's meddling and finding me a job, my old friends uninterested in doing anything other than smoking up, and Jay, still sitting on the porch, waiting for me, panic clawed at my throat. Will I lose everything I gained? Will I abandon the purpose I was discovering?

But then, I found Cole. And he reminded me that I can do both, that I can have it all. I just have to chase it, be open to it. I have an interview with Mel from the Art Attic this week. While the cupcake gig is a great option and I'd hang onto it for now, especially knowing Beau pulled strings to make it happen, there's no reason I can't teach pottery a few mornings or nights each week.

I love that Cole introduced me to the Art Attic. I love that he understands how important pottery is to me and is excited for my interview with Mel.

I trace my lips again, recalling that searing kiss that held so much promise. So much want and need and trust. Cole Philips is nothing like I expected when I moved home, but he's more than what I need. He's exactly what I want.

Pulling myself from bed, I ready for tonight's game. It feels different, going to The Honeycomb tonight. I'm not just going to sell cupcakes or cheer on Beau. Tonight, I'm also cheering for the man I want to call mine. And I hope, by the end of the night, that's exactly who he'll be.

My boyfriend, Cole. The Rookie.

"THESE ARE THE BEST CUPCAKES EVER!" A pre-teen girl grins at me, her braces flashing.

I smile back, loving her enthusiasm. "Try the apple strudel."

Her expression wavers.

Laughing, I pass her one. "I know, it sounds old-fashioned. But trust me, sometimes, the best things are the traditional ones."

Her mom gives me a thankful look as the girl bites into the cupcake. "Oh my God! This is incredible."

Her mom laughs. "Can I get four more of those?"

"Sure." I box the cupcakes and ring up their order.

They're the last customers in line from intermission and once they leave, I heave out a sigh of relief. I plop down on the barstool, catching my breath. The last thirty minutes have been crazy intense. Primrose Sweets pop-up was slammed with customers.

Buzzing with adrenaline, I can't believe I pulled it off. Now, glancing at the remaining six cupcakes, I realize what an incredible enterprise this concept is for Noelle and Scott. We're going to sell out.

"You're doing awesome, Bea," Noelle says, appearing in my peripheral vision.

I turn toward her, my mouth dropping open. "I had no idea you were here."

She laughs, leaning her hip against the ledge. "I flew in from Boston this afternoon to check in. I wanted to see you in action."

My face heats and I know my cheeks are bright red, matching my hair.

"You are flawless," Noelle reassures me. She enters the stand and pulls out two cupcakes, passing me one. "Great job tonight." She bumps her cupcake against mine. "And I've heard all positive things from everyone I talked to about your performance over the last month." She takes a huge bite of her cupcake while I watch her in awe. "It was awesome that you were able to start and run the stand during the hockey clinic."

Is she serious? People...noticed me? Think I'm doing a good job?

"Eat the cupcake," Noelle advises.

I shake myself out of it and take a bite, closing my eyes as the gooey chocolate fills my mouth. God, it's a masterpiece.

"I'm opening a few more pop-ups this year, mostly at arenas in the South."

My eyes open as I stare at Noelle. My mouth is filled with chocolate cupcake and I'm glad. Right now, I'd rather hear her out then comment.

"If you're looking for a more permanent position, I'll be filling a regional manager role soon. You can toss your name into the hat."

Wow. The fact that Noelle would consider me for such a position after a month fills me with pride. I may have gotten this gig because of Beau, but Noelle's consideration for a higher position is clearly rooted in my performance.

I swallow my cupcake. "Thank you, Noelle. Truly." I dip my head.

"But you still want to do your own thing."

I look up. "It's not that I'm not grateful," I rush to explain. "I just don't want to give up on my daydream."

"You shouldn't," she says, surprising me. "But, if you're serious about it, what's your plan?"

"My plan?"

"Yeah." She pours herself a cup of coffee. When she gestures to me, I shake my head. If I have coffee now, I'll be wired tonight at Corks. "How are you going to make your dream a reality?"

"I have an interview this week at the Art Attic," I admit. "It's for a teaching position for a pottery course. The class will be a few mornings a week, nothing that will interfere with my commitment here."

Noelle laughs, the sound musical. Her blonde ringlets bounce. "Relax, Bea. Primrose is my baby. I know it's not for everyone. A woman your age, with your talent, well, I'd be disappointed if you didn't want to take a shot at your dream. Tell me about the Art Attic."

I do. As Noelle and I clean and close down the pop-up shop, I tell her about pottery. I confide how much I love making vases, quirky pieces that tell a story. I tell her about the showcase I participated in in Nashville.

She listens attentively and asks a few questions. As we walk toward the rink, moving through a door that leads to boxed seats, my breath lodges in my throat.

Out on the ice, Cole blocks Miami's center, gaining control of the puck and flipping it to River Patton. My words die in my throat as I get caught up in the play.

Excitement hums through the arena. Fans are on their feet. River moves like flowing water, too fluid to catch. When he takes a shot, the puck soars into the top left-hand corner of the net and the crowd goes wild.

Scott Reland claps appreciatively. "Clean goal," he comments to someone. "But Philips, the rookie? He's got a future ahead of him."

Pride fills my chest that Scott Reland, owner of a powerhouse team, complimented Cole.

Next to me, Noelle bumps my shoulder. Turning toward her, I blush when I realize I stopped talking mid-sentence.

Amusement lines her face and she chuckles. "Whatever you do, Bea, don't give up your daydream for anyone." Her eyes cut back to the ice knowingly. I'm not sure if her gaze zeroes in on my brother or Cole but either way, her meaning is clear. I shouldn't let anyone hold me back from pursuing my passion.

Didn't Cole say the same thing?

I clear my throat. "Thanks, Noelle."

"When you set up shop, I'd love a vase."

I laugh. "Absolutely."

TEN
COLE

"THAT WAS one hell of a block, Rookie." Devon Hardt smacks me on the shoulder.

"You did good, kid," Brawler agrees, one corner of his mouth curling into an almost smile. He rarely gives a full one, well, unless he's with his woman, Maisy.

"Good game, Bolts." Coaches Noah Scotch and Jeremiah Merrick walk into the locker room, looking more at ease than they have for the first half of the season.

It hasn't been easy, buying a team, taking a new group of athletes and rebuilding every aspect of the Bolts from the ground up. But Scotch and Merrick have created a culture at the Bolts that's rooted in family. By extension, the management and the staff are supportive. They want us to succeed as players, as people, just as much as they want the team to get a bunch of W's. When I was in college, I heard stories about how difficult and competitive moving up to the league is. The Thunderbolts have been a happy surprise, providing a positive overall experience with invested coaches and high team morale.

"Nice work, Philips," Coach Merrick singles me out. A thrill rushes through my body, but I don't let it show. No one needs to know how badly I need that reassurance, that praise, that nod letting me know, *hey you're doing all right.* I've blocked out my past in nearly every way that counts except the most important one—failure isn't an option. *Prove them all wrong.*

The team cheers and I dip my head, grateful for their recognition. I don't take it for granted. No matter how many rungs on the ladder I climb, I'm still more scared of slipping down a peg than reaching the next one. I keep my head down, put in the work, and give every practice, every game, everything I got.

Tonight, it paid off. Tonight only, I'll let myself enjoy the moment, this feeling. I'll allow myself to get swept up by the camaraderie of my team, the celebratory bustle at Corks, and the beautiful smile of Bea Turner.

Did she see my block? Did she clap and cheer with the rest of the stadium? I hope so.

The team settles down. Our coaches point out a few things we could have done differently and offer a glimpse of what practice will look like this week. Then, we're dismissed.

I shower quickly, desperate to get out of the locker room and see if Bea stuck around. She hasn't messaged me, so I hope she's waiting. I hope she wants to head to Corks together. I hope tonight is the night I can tell her I want this to be legit. I want to be her man and I want to show up for her.

"You heading to Corks?" Beau asks as I close my locker door.

I narrow my eyes at him. There's no way Bea told him about us. If she did, he'd say something to me. Instead, he's acting affable and slightly aloof, the way he always is. Shit, is she having second thoughts? Is tonight not the night I get to tell my team I'm with Bea? I clear my throat. "Yeah, man."

He taps my shoulder. "See you there. I gotta catch up with my sister. She wanted to talk." He shrugs and relief fills my chest.

Does she want to tell him about us? Is it better or worse for him to learn this news after a win and before a night at a bar? Will he care? After the initial surprise, I can't see how Beau will mind my dating Bea. I treat women, hell I treat strangers, well. My word is my word and I only give my best to the relationships I foster.

Probably why I don't foster many but still...

"See you there." I wave goodbye.

My phone beeps and I tug it from my pocket.

BEA

Hey! CONGRATS ON YOUR WIN! That block was incredible. (Fire emoji) Catching a ride with Beau so we can talk. See you at Corks! (Heart emoji)

I blow out an exhale and bite back my smile. Bea is going to talk to Beau and meet me at the bar. Then, we'll have several things to celebrate. As great as tonight's win feels, it feels even better knowing I'm going to make this thing with Bea real.

Squaring my shoulders, I head out to the parking lot and drive to Corks, riding a wave of adrenaline from the game mixed with anticipation for tonight.

CORKS IS PACKED. Over the past few months, as the Thunderbolts began to play decent hockey, we've started drawing a larger crowd. A bigger fanbase. It's spilled over into the town bars and now, when we enter Corks after a game, there's a few guys either buying our drinks or calling us out for poor plays.

Happily, tonight is the former.

"Hell of a block, Rookie!" A guy pats me on the back as I pass.

"Thanks." I grin. While some of my teammates, mostly Devon, are used to the fanfare, it's new to me.

But I like it. I enjoy knowing that I've earned someone's respect through the quality of my game. It's the one thing I set out to do, and knowing I'm living up to my own expectations, achieving my goals, never gets old.

When I step to the bar, I gesture that I'll buy a round, but Brawler's hand darts out. He taps my wrist. "Your first drink is on me, Rookie. You earned it."

"Thanks, Brawler." I keep the emotion out of my tone. I don't let him see that inside, I'm lit up like a meteor shower. The last thing I want is for my team to think I'm getting a big head, that an inflated ego is going to lead to an unfocused player. I order a beer, knowing I'll nurse it the entire night.

No way in hell do I want to be drunk, or even tipsy, when I have the talk I want to have with Bea. Tonight, I need to make sure we're on the same page and taking the next step together.

I check my watch. What's taking Turner so long? Is he pissed about me seeing Bea? Does he feel blindsided that I didn't talk to him about it? Should I have—even though I didn't know Bea was his sister when I first met her?

The door to Corks opens and I spot my beautiful lioness. A smile cracks my face, too big to pass off as anything but delight. Bea's eyes search for me. As soon as she spots me, she moves in my direction.

I step toward her, as if pulled by an invisible thread. Beau's eyes narrow at his sister's side, but I ignore him. Right now, I don't want to look at anyone but the beautiful woman I want to build a future with.

Hyped up on tonight's game, on the praise I received, on the buzz of Corks, I can't stop myself from reaching for Bea.

"Cole, I—" she says as I tug her against my chest.

Damn, I want to kiss this beautiful girl. I shake my head, bewitched by the shades of grey and slate, pewter and silver, in her expressive eyes. Dropping my mouth, I kiss her hard, so damn happy she's here, with me, tonight.

Bea whimpers and I grow rock fucking hard at the sound. How does one kiss affect her so deeply? How does one moan make me want to pick her up and leave Corks behind?

My arm is ripped back, and I'm swung around. I throw my other arm out, intent on defending Bea from whatever the hell is going on. What idiot is—

Beau Turner's angry face, wild eyes and twisted mouth, greets me. "What the fuck, Rookie?"

"What?" I shake my head.

Turner grips the collar of my shirt, clenching it in his fists as he shoves me backward, through a sea of people until my back collides with the bar.

Brawler's on his feet. Devon is in Beau's face.

"Calm the fuck down, man," Devon says.

I shake my head. "What's wrong—"

"No!" Beau shakes his head. "What the fuck is wrong with you? Why the fuck are your hands on my sister?"

Shit. I close my eyes. She didn't tell him.

"Beau, Beau, please." Bea tugs on Beau's arm, her tone pleading. "Let me explain."

Beau doesn't spare her a glance. His gaze is hard and unyielding, pinned to mine.

"Oh shit!" River calls out. "The Rookie is screwing Turner's sister. You gonna let that shit stand, Turner?"

I swear, Patton needs to be decked in the mouth. Repeatedly.

"Beau! Listen to me," Bea tries again.

"I care about her, man," I say, cutting to the chase.

Bea stops jumping up and down. Her eyes cut to mine. Our corner of the bar quiets down as confusion passes through Turner's eyes.

"You don't even know her. Fuck, she's been back a month." He shakes his head, and then, another thought moves over his face. "Wait, how long has this shit been going on?"

"Beau!" Bea calls. She pinches her brother so hard that he snaps his head toward hers. She's furious now. Her cheeks are bright red, her eyes blazing. She's morphing into a lioness before my eyes and she's so fucking gorgeous, brilliant, I can't tear my eyes away. "Outside. Right now."

River whistles low.

Beau shakes his head again. Bea kicks him in the shin.

"Ow!" Beau cries out. "Are you—"

"Outside. Now," she says it again. Her voice cracks like a whip and Brawler looks impressed.

Beau sighs. He tightens his grip on my shirt and gives it a little shake. "After I talk to my sister, I'm coming for you, Rookie. You better be right fucking here."

I grin, half amused, half annoyed. "I look forward to it, Turner."

"Jesus," Devon mutters, annoyed. His girlfriend, Mila, looks like she's holding back laughter.

Maisy Stratford looks worried.

River fucking cackles. "This just keeps getting better."

"Shh!" Maisy quiets him.

River shuts his mouth by draining half a beer.

I turn away from my team and watch Bea walk through Corks. Everyone gets out of her way, as if she's parting the sea, and I can't help but smile.

There's my girl, my lioness.

WHEN BEA COMES BACK into Corks, I'm nursing the same beer. The team has given me a wide birth. Other than

Maisy Stratford, who finds my blossoming romance with Bea swoon-worthy, no one else has commented.

I mean, River Patton's got a lot to say, but he's not directing any of it to me. Just running his mouth, like usual.

I stand as soon as I spot Bea cutting her way to the bar. Her cheeks are red, but her eyes are clear and relief snakes through me that she didn't cry. I'd hate if her talk with Beau left her in tears and I don't want to be angry with one of my teammates if it can be avoided. I'd be fucking furious if Beau made Bea cry and that's a new feeling for me to process.

I don't do furious; I put in work and get results.

"Hey," I say softly when Bea steps into my arms. Her hands find purchase on my biceps and she looks up at me, soulful grey eyes and an adorable, red-tipped nose. "You okay?"

"Yeah," she says, glancing over her shoulder at Beau. "I think I hurt his feelings."

"By not telling him?" I guess, understanding the heart of it. If I found out Jamie was dating one of my teammates and hadn't told me, I'd be hurt too. Upset with her but pissed as fuck with my teammate.

Bea nods and I brush her hair away from her face. I cut a look to Beau who is glaring at me, waiting by the door that lets out to a side entrance and porch. Yep, he's angry with me.

I roll back my shoulders. Whatever. He can be pissed off and we can have words, as long as this shit doesn't touch Bea. And, for her, I'll smooth it over.

I squeeze her shoulders and place a kiss to the crown of her head. "Let me talk to him." I tip my head toward the side entrance. "What are you drinking?"

She lets out a sigh. When her eyes travel down the bar and spot Mila and Maisy, she relaxes a little. I don't think Bea's ever met them, but I know Mila and Mais will go out of their way to make her feel comfortable.

When she has an IPA in hand, I take her hand and walk her over to Mila and Maisy.

"Mila, Mais, this is Bea," I say, running my palm over Bea's back to relax her.

"Hi, Bea, I'm Mila." Mila extends a hand.

"It's great to meet you!" Maisy says enthusiastically. She boots River from his barstool to make room for Bea.

As Bea slips onto the stool and gives me a smile, I relax a little, knowing she's in good hands. Then, I stride toward Beau.

He shakes his head when I'm within hearing range. "Can't fucking believe you."

"Outside," I say, my body oscillating between burning and freezing. My stomach feels funny, my chest too tight. I fucking hate confrontation. I hate anything that has the potential to dissolve into a fight, to get messy. But I need to step up for Bea, show her and her brother, show everyone in Corks, that I'm serious about her.

I can't do that without clearing the air with Beau.

Beau and I step onto the side porch at Corks. His hands are balled into fists. Wary eyes and a slashed mouth.

I sigh. "I care about her, Beau."

He looks out over the parking lot, his anger radiating from his shoulders. It shimmers in the air around him, as if he's coiled too tight, going to explode at any moment.

For the first time, I wonder what Beau's time in the military was like. I know he served in Afghanistan but what demons, what shadows, losses and hurts, did he carry home with him?

"Why didn't you tell me?" His voice is low.

"Last night was our first real date," I admit. "I attempted Beef Wellington. It burned."

His eyes cut back to mine, more curious now.

"I didn't know she was your sister when I met her. At the cupcake stand. Your gran spilled the beans."

"You met Gran?" His body language shifts toward me, arms crossed over his chest. "I mean, aside from your birthday. You went to Gran's house?"

"Yes. Bea and I had lunch last week. Casual, still feeling each other out. But I knew from the moment I met her that I like her. I didn't know she was your sister."

"But then you did. And you still didn't say shit."

"Come on, Turner. Having lunch hardly constitutes dating. I wasn't going to talk to you about anything until I talked to your sister about it first. Last night, she said she wanted to talk to you. I respect the hell out of Bea and I'm following her lead. You guys are family. Don't take out your anger with me on her."

"I would never," he seethes.

"Good." I clear my throat, yank the back of my neck. My skin feels too tight, itchy and uncomfortable. "Bea wanted to talk to you about it. Today, before the game."

He hangs his head and I sense the regret he feels at not hearing her out earlier. "I took a call from a buddy, just re-upped."

"For the Marines?"

Beau nods and looks up. The agony burning in his eyes cuts through me. I don't know what Beau went through, but at his visible pain, it's clear he's still processing.

"I never intended to keep anything from you. Bea and me, we're still figuring it out. But I care about Bea. I respect her. And I want whatever the hell she'll give me."

He clears his throat, heaving out a sigh. Then, he sticks out his hand. "I get it. I didn't mean to jump to conclusions. Fucking hate being kept in the dark."

I smack my hand in his, shake. "I get it, Turner. But you need to trust Bea. She's smart and talented. More than capable of making her own decisions and looking out for herself."

He snorts. "You have a sister, Cole?"

"Yeah," I say, thinking of Jamie. "A cousin but we were raised like siblings."

"What would you do if the situation was reversed?"

I lift my chin in agreement. "Same as you."

"Good man." He smacks the center of my back. "Come on, I'll buy you a beer."

I chuckle and fall in step with him; we reenter Corks. "Only having the one tonight, Beau."

He cuts me a look.

"I'm taking your sister home." My intent is clear, my tone direct.

"Fuck," Beau mutters. "Spare me the details." He steps to the bar and orders a round.

But he exchanges a smile and a nod with his sister. When Bea looks at me, her eyes are clear, the corners of her mouth curling into a grin.

She's my girl.

ELEVEN

BEA

COLE FLIPS the ignition on his car and turns to face me.

"You're dropping me off at home," I muse, staring up at Gran's house.

He smiles. "No need to rush this, Bea. I meant what I said. This, you, mean something to me."

It's hard to argue with that. The man isn't taking me home and laying me down because he respects me. But does he have to respect me so much?

His hand slips over the steering wheel. "And I gotta get up and run in a few hours."

"Run? But you won tonight."

He chuckles. "Training doesn't pause because you win. You have to keep showing up."

A tiny flicker of shame burns through me that I'd rather he skip his run. I shift in the passenger seat, turning toward him. My thighs clench together and my heart gallops. I've never had such a visceral reaction to a man before, not even Jay, not even when we were together. I *want* Cole.

The way he stood up for us to my brother made me feel like I'm worth something priceless. When Beau returned from their talk, he grinned. Cole placed his hand on my back and leaned into the conversation I was having with Axel and Maisy.

Whatever transpired on the porch was positive. I don't know the details, but I know Cole wasn't crude or aggressive. If he was, Beau would have let his temper fly and Cole would have come back with a busted nose or split lip. Instead, Cole must have handled things maturely, with understanding. Like a real man.

"How did your talk with Beau go?" I ask, wanting the details.

"Fine," he admits, shrugging. "I think he felt caught off guard more than anything."

"Yeah," I admit. "Beau hates not knowing things. He hates feeling like he was excluded or like the wool is being pulled over his eyes. For so long, sometimes even now, he's more like a dad than my brother."

"I get that. Trust me, I've been there with Jamie. It sucks when you feel like a woman you love is being taken advantage of. But I'm not trying to take advantage of you, Bea. Or of this." He gestures between us. "I want to give us a real chance. I want you to be my girlfriend and I wanna be your man. I don't know if labels are even a thing anymore." His eyes flash, a chuckle falling from his mouth. "I've never been in a real romantic relationship before."

My eyes nearly fall out of my face. "Ever?"

Cole laughs again, the tips of his ears reddening. "Nah. It's always been hockey for me. I need to warn you, I'm not very good at balancing things. Hockey has been my life for as long as I can remember. Other than my cousin and uncle, my social circle has only ever consisted of my team. I've never partied or dated tons of women. I've always kept my head down and did what I needed to do to improve my game."

"And you want to take me on?" I half joke. "I'm a secret lioness, you know."

Cole smiles. "I want whatever you'll give me, Bea. But yeah, I want you to be my girl. Will you?"

"Yes," I say, giddiness filling my chest like laughing gas. "Yes, Cole, I want this too."

Cole gives me the most brilliant, radiant smile before pulling me over the center console. He meets me halfway and his mouth crashes over mine, kissing me with an edge that wasn't there before.

He claims me. I love knowing he's never shared this—parts of him—with any other woman before. He's opening up to me, confiding in me, and I'm too swept up in him to dwell on anything but the moment.

Our kiss turns steamy. Cole's hands drag up from my shoulders, cupping my cheeks. His long fingers tangle in my curls, angling my head as my tongue dances with his. My nipples tighten, my thighs press together.

I want to vault myself over the center console and sit in his lap. I want to press my body into his and let him feel exactly what he does to me. He consumes me, makes me reckless in a way that's more delicious than dangerous.

When Cole's hand falls away from my cheek, brushes my shoulder, and softly caresses my breast, I whimper. I push up onto my knees and crawl into his lap, straddling him.

He pulls away, shock crossing his face. "Bea."

"Just kiss me, Cole," I practically whimper. I don't care how needy I appear. Because I do need him. I *want* him.

A growl rips from Cole's throat and he's on me. His hands moving over my heated skin, his tongue in my mouth. Then his lips are on my neck, I'm gripping his hair, my body involuntarily grinding over his.

"Jesus, Bea," he moans. "We gotta slow down, beautiful. I want you so fucking badly but not like this. Not in my car in your gran's driveway."

Gran! "Shit!" I sit up, my ass bumping the steering wheel

and causing a short, loud horn to blast. I blush furiously as Cole grins.

"You think she's waiting by the window, don't you?"

"She's one-hundred percent spying on us," I lament, wishing I wasn't speaking the truth.

Cole, instead of the sweet, kinda shy guy I'm getting to know, laughs. He shakes his head and fixes my disheveled shirt before his one hand palms my ass. "You're my girl, Bea?"

"I'm your girl, Cole."

He leans closer and presses one deep, soul-searching kiss against my lips. "Sleep well, beautiful. I'll call you in the morning."

I beam at him, my body feeling like Jell-O. What is it about Cole that turns me into mush? I want to melt into him, seep into his skin, and stay with him for the rest of the night. His hand taps my ass and I pull myself from his hard, delectable, grind-worthy body.

When I'm back in the passenger seat, Cole exits the car and rounds the front to my door. He pulls it open for me, extends his hand, and like the gentleman he is, bids me good night on the front porch.

The lights flicker on and off three times, a warning from Gran. We both laugh, the two of us encapsulated in this bubble of giddy happiness, of pure joy. It's too good and too funny for me to be embarrassed so I kiss my boyfriend one more time before slipping inside.

"You're lucky we live in the country, girl," Gran says the moment I cross the threshold. She's seated in a rocker by the window, a Bible in her lap. "You would have given the whole neighborhood a show. Pay. Per. View."

Tossing my head back, I laugh. "I love you, Gran."

Gran shakes her head, but her eyes are gleaming.

Tonight was one of the best nights I've ever had. I shower

and change for bed. When I slip underneath the sheets, I close my eyes and dream about my boyfriend.

"WE'RE delighted to welcome you to our team." Mel stands and shakes my hand.

"I'm thrilled to begin. Thank you so much for this opportunity," I say.

"Come on, I'll show you your workspace." Mel walks me to a nearby studio and stands back as I enter the space.

My eyes run over the tools and equipment. The massive windows letting in natural light. The various types of clay, the colors, the spinning wheels. It's a much larger version of my she-shed and I love that I can spend as much time as I want sculpting here. Creating and envisioning and shaping.

I take a deep breath, excited to dive into my position. "I can't wait to help others find their passion, their outlet, with this type of work. Working with your hands to create is so satisfying."

"It is," Mel agrees. "I'm happy you're joining us, Bea."

"Me too." I smile at her.

Mel leaves me to get situated in the space. I spend my afternoon taking stock of the supplies—they have everything —and outlining the first series of courses I'd like to offer. By the time I finish, it's dusk and I've missed a slew of calls and messages.

COLE

Morning, beautiful girl. How did it go with Mel?

BEAU

Hey, want to get lunch this week?

JAY

I miss you, Bea. Dad's been asking for you.
Come by the house this week? Just to hang
out, I swear.

COLE

Hey! Let me know if you got the gig (I'm sure
you did).

CELINE

YOUR RELATIONSHIP STATUS? I need an
update...

BODHI

Yo! I'm coming in early for Gran's birthday.
Pencil me in for a dinner.

COLE

Bea? I'm getting worried...

COLE

Babe, I'm heading into the gym. I'll call you
after. I hope you're okay.

BEAU

Hey?? You okay? Haven't heard from you
today...

Guilt swells in my chest that I caused Cole and Beau to worry. I lost track of time, immersed in my happy place. On my way out, I wave to Mel. I'll email her my outline tonight.

Once I slide into my car, I call Cole. It goes to voicemail and I realize he's probably at the gym. Next, I call Beau.

"Hey!" He answers on the first ring. "You okay? I've been messaging you."

"Yes, I know. I got a job!" I blurt out.

"What?" He sounds confused.

"The Art Attic," I say, explaining my new position as an instructor.

"Wow, Bea, that's amazing." I can hear the pride in Beau's

voice, and it fills me with excitement. Maybe he'll understand how important starting my own business is. Maybe this job is the first step in proving that I'm capable of having a career in the art world. "Are you still going to stay at Primrose?"

Meh, maybe not. I clear my throat, not wanting to make Beau look bad with Noelle and Scott by quitting. Guilt swims in my stomach at the thought, even though logically, I know my time with Primrose is winding down. I clear my throat. "Of course."

"Good," he says, his relief evident. "Well, want to get a bite? Dinner? We should celebrate."

"I'd love to," I say quickly, touched by his offer. "Hey, do you need to be working out right now?"

"What?" He laughs. "Definitely not. We had a morning lift and a grueling practice."

"Oh." Why would Cole need to work out again after such an intense day? *Training doesn't pause because you win.*

"Why?" Beau asks.

I worry my bottom lip between my teeth. "Cole mentioned hitting the gym."

Beau snickers. "Yeah, well, Cole is an animal. The kid is in the gym, hitting the weights, 24/7. I swear he trains the way most people breathe, nonstop."

"Right," I say. Cole already told me this and yet, a small part of me is disappointed that he's not around right now to celebrate my good news. It's not fair since I missed his calls and messages all day. I know that. Shaking my head, I clear the thought away. "Where do you want to get dinner?"

"Feel like coming to Knoxville?"

"Now?"

"It's only forty minutes, Bea."

I glance down at my outfit. I dressed up today, in a cute linen skirt and blouse, for my interview. I can fix my hair and makeup in the car… "I'm on my way."

"Sweet! See you soon."

I disconnect with Beau and get on the road. Halfway into my drive, Cole calls.

"Hey, you," I answer via the Bluetooth.

"Hey! How'd it go?" He asks about my interview right away and I love that he's been thinking about it, about me, all day.

"I got the job!"

"Of course, you did. We should celebrate."

My earlier frustration fades away at his excitement. "I'd love to but I'm on my way to Knoxville to have dinner with Beau."

"Oh, nice. That's great, Bea." There's no frustration or jealousy in Cole's tone. Instead, he's genuinely happy for me to spend time with my brother. It's a reality check because Jay always grumbled when I spent too much time with my brothers. He would say I was neglecting him.

"Thanks! Can we celebrate this weekend?"

"We will more than celebrate this weekend," Cole laughs. "I promise."

"Okay."

"Message or call when you get home, okay? Or let me know if you need a ride."

I snort. The thing is, I know he's serious. He would drive all the way to Knoxville to come pick me up without a second thought. "I'll be fine, Cole. But I'll message you before I sleep."

"Okay. Have fun, babe."

"'Bye." I end the call and change lanes.

I drive the rest of the way on cloud nine. I'm finally reconnecting with my brother. I'm starting a dream job, in my field. And I've got the best boyfriend in the world. Does it get any better than this?

TWELVE
COLE

I WAS ON FIRE TONIGHT. Four blocks, three assists, a big, fat fucking win. Adrenaline is still pounding through my veins when I leave the locker room. I'm on a streak and it feels good. I've worked hard for this, to be an asset to my team. To show Merrick and Scotch that betting on me was a good call.

"You were amazing!" Bea squeals when she sees me.

I don't break my pace, just scoop her into my arms and head toward the exit.

"What the fuck's got into the rookie?" Damien Barnes hollers.

"Turner's sister," River remarks.

"Watch that shit," I hear Brawler tell him.

Normally, the comment would pull me up short. But not tonight. I don't have time for fucking Patton and his antics.

Whistles and cheers break out behind me, but I tune them out. I don't turn around because Bea is laughing, her breathless giggle washing over my ear. Her legs wind around my abdomen as she clutches my shoulders to hang on. Her breasts press into my chest, her scent tickles my nose, and my blood heats.

Jesus, I want her. I can't wait any longer. All week, I've been hopped up on energy. Coiled too tight, in desperate need of a release I've never experienced before. It goes beyond hockey. I spend most of my free time in the gym, but this week, extra workouts didn't cut it. Nothing tired me out the way my body craves.

Then, I figured it out. "Fucking need you, Bea," I growl as I reach my car. I release her, her body sliding down mine.

She gasps as she feels my erection, already hard and straining against my sweats at the mere thought of finally getting her into my bed. I didn't want to rush shit. I want her to know how much she means to me. Does she? Does she have any idea the depths of things I feel for her? It hasn't been a long time, but I know, deep down, she's the woman for me.

"Then take me home, Cole."

I watch her carefully. "You sure? I—"

"I'm ready. I'm sure."

"Me too." I pull open her door, silently tossing up a prayer to the heavens.

Then, I drive us to my home and invite Bea into my bed, into my life, and all the way into my heart.

She comes willingly. The rounded dip of her shoulders is gone. The shyness that shows in the way she hides herself disappears. My lioness emerges, certain and wanting.

It's the hottest thing I've ever seen, Bea bathed in confidence.

"You were on fire tonight," she tells me as she lifts her arms.

I drag her shirt up and over her head, dropping it to the floor.

"I was hoping you watched."

"I caught the last three minutes," she admits. I know she was working the cupcake stand and that, as usual, she was slammed with customers. Still, I love knowing that she caught some of the game. It was intense and nonstop, but tonight, I had the spark. The speed. I'm continuing my streak.

It feels almost as good as this moment, when Bea pushes my sweats down my legs and I lose my shirt.

I roll her jeans down her legs next and she kicks them off. We're facing each other, rocking only our undergarments, and still, we haven't kissed.

The tension builds as Bea drinks in my body. As my eyes kiss every inch of her skin. When we can't handle it any longer, we spring toward each other. I catch her around the waist and my mouth meets hers, hot and greedy. Her hands knead my hips, track along my back, her nails sinking into the skin.

Hissing, I pull back, but Bea is on me, climbing up my body, her mouth dragging over my shoulder, her heels hooking behind my back.

"Fuck, Bea." I lay her down in the center of my bed and crawl over her. She arches up, drawing me closer, until our lips meet again.

Our frantic edge softens into deep, sensual kisses. Bea sucks on my tongue as I pop the clasp on her bra. When her bare breasts, pale pink nipples, come into view, my throat dries. "You're so beautiful, Bea. So fucking gorgeous." Bending my neck, I take one breast into my mouth, my hand moving down to massage between her legs.

Her breathing picks up as I push her underwear to the side. My fingers drag through her arousal. "So fucking wet." I smear it over her clit. Bea lifts her hips to meet my movement and I shower her other breast with attention. My fingers are coated with her need, my cock rock fucking solid against her thigh.

I should be worried about rushing this. I should try to slow it down. But with Bea, I can't. I'm along for the ride and this one is the best I've ever been on.

As Bea's hands roam over my body, gripping my arms,

moving along my back, I slide two fingers inside of her. She gasps, her eyes fluttering closed. I pump my fingers slowly, unable to tear my eyes away from her expression.

It's beatific, coated in bliss and trust. "You're killing me, Cole," she murmurs.

I press my thumb to her clit. "You're killing me, Bea. So gorgeous."

Bea's eyes pop open, an edge of panic in them. "Cole," she murmurs. I realize she's close to orgasming. I drop down beside her, curling my arm around her protectively and drawing her into my chest. I kiss her cheeks, her eyelids, her forehead. But my hand between her legs never stops moving.

"Cole," she whimpers.

"I got you, Bea. Come for me, baby."

My words are her undoing. Her pussy clenches around my fingers before she cries out my name, riding the wave of bliss, her expression wavering between awe and joy.

"It's never been like that before."

"Then he wasn't doing it right," I say softly.

Bea shakes her head. "I didn't know, I didn't realize it could be that good."

"Always, Bea," I promise to always make it good for her.

She stares at me for so long, I'm tempted to ask if she wants to call it a night. It would give me the worst case of blue balls in the history of mankind, but I don't want to pressure her. If she's never had a real orgasm before, I don't want to be a dick and push for more. But then she swings a leg over my torso and props herself up, her hands planting on my chest. "My turn."

I grin, turned on by the wicked gleam in her eyes. "What does your turn entail?"

"You'll see," she says coyly, her shyness gone.

Bea moves down my body slowly, pressing kisses along my abdomen, until she comes eye to eye with my cock. For a moment, I wonder if she needs me to walk her through it, but then, her lips clamp around my length and I see fucking stars. Her hand fists my cock, her mouth licks and sucks, alternating the pressure, and my mind shuts down.

I can't think about anything except Bea. My fingers lace through her hair. Glancing down, the visual of Bea sucking me off is one I'll recall for the rest of my life. It's the hottest thing I've ever witnessed. Her red hair is like fire in my hands. Her mouth feels like perfection on my cock. But her sounds, the tiny mewls and moans she makes, lift me higher and higher until I'm gripping her hair. "Baby, stop. You keep doing that, I'm going to come."

"So come," she tosses it out like a challenge.

I laugh, the sound scraping out of my throat. "I'd rather be inside you."

She gives me a smart-ass look.

Pulling her up my frame, I kiss her hard before rolling us over.

Bea gasps when she lands underneath me. Reaching over, I pull a condom out of my bedside drawer—the box was a housewarming gift from Devon—and roll it on.

Then, I position myself at her entrance. My eyes hold hers. Soft grey and excited silver. "You sure, baby?"

"Please, Cole," she nearly begs.

I push inside of her and swear. "Jesus, you're fucking perfect."

She laughs but it fades away the moment I begin to move. Instead, I rock into her, she holds on to me, and we build the most beautiful crescendo, until we both peak and free-fall.

I pull Bea into my arms and hold her against my chest as we lie in sated bliss. I kiss her forehead, brushing sweaty tendrils of hair away from her face. "You okay?"

"I'm wonderful."

I snort. "Me too."

"It's never been like that for me."

"For me either," I admit. "I think it's the emotional aspect, makes everything more intense." I link our hands together. "I know it hasn't been long, Bea. But I've never felt this way about a woman before."

She squeezes my hand. "Me neither."

"I don't want to mess this up with you." I kiss her forehead.

"You won't. I want you to meet my family, Cole." She lifts her chin to gauge my reaction.

"I'd love to." I mean it too. Uncle Kirk and Jamie mean everything to me. I know if I had a family like Bea's, with a bunch of siblings, I'd be hounding her to meet them.

She smiles. "Will you be my date to Gran's birthday party next month?"

I smile back, leaning over to kiss her lips. "I'll be your forever date, Bea."

She sighs contentedly. "I hope so, Cole."

Me too.

THE NEXT MORNING, it's hard as hell to pull myself from bed. With Bea's naked body tangled in the sheets, the last thing I feel like doing is going for a run, followed by a lift.

But I've made a commitment to the Bolts. I made a commitment to myself. So, before the sun rises, I kiss Bea's naked shoulder and slip from the bed. I tug on a hoodie and pop in my EarPods.

Then, I take off for a sunrise run, pounding the pavement with all the pent-up energy still stored in my bloodstream. Last night was one of the best nights of my life.

Bea's scent clings to my skin and her sweet moans ring in my ears. For the first time in my life, there's something other than hockey to contend with. I don't want to ever let her down. I always want to be enough for her.

For sure, it will be tough to balance a relationship with my commitment to hockey. But I'm nothing if not dedicated. Determined.

I just need to work harder to make sure I'm the best player I can possibly be when I glide out onto the ice. And the best boyfriend to Bea always. Her disappointment would wreck me just as much as having a shitty game.

The realization should scare me. It should serve as a wake-up call that it's going to be tough, downright grueling, to simultaneously excel in both areas.

Instead, it motivates the hell out of me, and I pick up the pace, setting my fastest mile time this season. If you want something good, you have to work for it.

Prove them all wrong.

THIRTEEN
BEA

I'M WASHING the tools from my first pottery class, a thrill of satisfaction rippling through my body, when I hear the door creak open.

Turning to look over my shoulder, I frown when Jay enters the space.

"What are you doing here, Jay?" I turn off the faucet and grab a paper towel.

His eyes scan my frame. Messy, unruly curls held back by a thick hairband. Bits of dried clay dotting my arms. An old smock, the color of red wine, wrapping around my body. I raise my eyebrows.

"You look like you used to," he says softly, confusion in his eyes. "What happened to us, Bea?" Jay takes a chair and sits down, crossing one foot over his knee.

I sigh. I knew this was coming. There's no way Jay understood any of my attempts to redirect our relationship into a friendship, not really. He truly believed that I needed time to process my move and then we'd fall back into our old selves. A self I haven't been for almost five years.

Still, it pains me to see someone I've spent years loving, an adolescence caring about, hurting. It aches to know I'm the cause of it. Jay and I may not have much in common anymore, we may not want the same things, but he's not a bad guy. He's a wounded one.

I take the seat across from him. "Jay, we had an amazing high school relationship. You were my first everything and that's special. It's—"

"Then why do you want to throw it away?"

"It's not enough anymore." The words feel like warbled rocks dropping from my mouth, but they need to be said. I need Jay to *listen* to me, not just hear me. "I'm with Cole now."

He scoffs, his eyes flaring with jealousy.

The years I was at art school, I know Jay dated. High school friends, social media profiles, whenever he went on a date, it would make its way back to me. Truly, I was happy for him. Relieved even, that he was moving on. But he never moved on. He never took the next step. He always kept it casual, a handful of dates that meant a fun night out and maybe a morning coffee.

One of our mutual friends from high school told me as much when I was home over Christmas break. She hinted that I'd need to be stern with Jay, that he was still waiting for me. At the time, I thought she was exaggerating. Now, I realize she's right.

While Jay waited, I tried to grow and evolve. To figure out the kind of life I want to lead and the people I want to surround myself with. For sure, it's pottery and art. And now, it's Cole. He pushes me to be a better version of myself, to reach for my dreams and turn them into goals. Attainable, achievable goals. Looking around the space I'm sitting in, it's already happening.

Sure, I would have found the Art Attic eventually. But Cole brought me here, encouraged me to talk to Mel, celebrated when I earned the position. Tonight, he's taking me to my favorite gelateria in Knoxville to celebrate my first class.

He cares about things I care about not because he has an interest in them but because they're important to me. And I'm important to him.

"Bea?"

I look up and realize by Jay's expression that he must have said my name several times.

I shake my head to clear it. "Yeah?"

"Are you his girlfriend?"

"Yes."

Jay shoots up from his chair, as if manually ejected. His hands rake through his hair. "And you think it's for real?"

I shrug. "I want to find out."

"Unbelievable," he mutters, shaking his head. "You finally come home and just cast me aside because a flashy—"

"I'm falling in love with him." My tone is like steel. I stand from my chair, much calmer than I feel. Holy shit, I'm falling in love with him. I hadn't meant to blurt out the words, and certainly not to Jay before Cole, but…they're true. The moment I say them, I know it in my bones.

I'm falling in love with Cole Philips.

Is it possible to fall for someone so quickly? I think of my parents, their whirlwind romance, the five children they bore, the love they showered us with. Of course, it is. In fact, Mom would probably say I was fortunate, blessed, to be certain in my feelings for Cole. I smile but quickly bite my lip when I see the agony that blazes over Jay's expression.

"I'm sorry, Jay. I never meant to hurt you. When we dated, we were in high school. You were all I knew before I moved to Nashville. In that time, I changed. We don't have a future. Not anymore."

Jay looks at me for a long moment, the intensity in his gaze searing. He stares like he doesn't even recognize me. I remain still, calm, even though my heart is galloping.

Then, without warning, he reaches out and grasps my

wrists. Holding them tightly, he shakes me. "You're going to regret this, Bea."

"Let go of me, Jay. Now," I demand, an edge of hysteria in my tone. Jay's never tried to hurt me before. He's never threatened me. But I'd be lying if I said there weren't moments when I thought he *could*. Right now, those old fears resurface. Looking into his eyes, I see his anger, the betrayal he feels, and it frightens me.

I pull my arms from his grasp and he swears. The haze in his eyes clears and remorse fills them. "Shit!" He shakes his head, apology written in his expression. "Shit, Bea, I'm sorry," his voice cracks.

Then, he stalks from the space, the door closing behind him. It rings with a finality that fills me with relief. I sink back to the chair and let out an uneven breath. What the hell just happened?

I glance down at the red links cuffing my wrists. What was Jay thinking?

My adrenaline subsides even though my thoughts rush. Should I tell Cole? Beau? Anyone? Or is it finally handled?

I sit for a long time, staring into space, getting my breathing under control.

Today, a new chapter opened with my first course. Another one closed, long overdue, between Jay and me. It's done.

My phone beeps.

COLE

How is ice cream as a girlfriend??

I roll my eyes. Cole's message injects lightness back into my day, making the exchange with Jay feel like it was hours ago. Like it doesn't even matter.

BEA

How?

COLE

The sweetest.

BEA

Aww (heart eyes emoji)

COLE

Pick you up at 6 PM.

BEA

Can't wait!

COLE

Me too. Wanna hear all about your class.

BEA

XO

I push Jay out of my mind completely. Then, I slip my phone into my purse, do one last check of the studio, and take a deep breath. It feels like today marks the start of my adulthood, of my real life.

I'm excited to greet it. With an ice cream cone and the man I'm falling in love with.

IT'S good that Cole and I squeeze in an ice cream date because the two weeks that follow are a whirlwind.

Cole's commitment to training is next-level intense. He wakes up early to run, he adds lifts to the team's workouts, and he's the first at the rink, last to leave, for nearly every practice. Factor in his travel time, away games, and the mental space he likes to get into before home games, and I barely see him.

But also, I have my own things going on. Besides the part-time hours I'm working at Primrose, I'm now teaching four mornings and one rotating evening a week at the Art Attic.

My time there is sacred, pulling me into a world where my thoughts cease, my stress fades away, and my hands create. I lose hours in the studio, fully invested in whatever I'm working on. Usually, it's vases. But I started a new mug series and some bowls.

I want to prove to Mel that I can teach additional courses. I want to prove to myself that I can launch a business and flourish, professionally and personally, in this industry. Next month, when Bodhi comes up for Gran's party, I'm going to pitch him the business plan I've been working on. He's made his tattoo parlor the most sought-after place to get inked in Miami Beach. If anyone can put holes in my plan, it's Bodhi and I know he'll take my desire to start a business as seriously as I do. Even if he warns me off it at the same time.

A knock sounds on the studio door and I turn, a ball of dread forming in my stomach when I recall how Jay showed up two weeks ago. I haven't heard from him since that day, and while a part of me thinks he finally got the message, another part of me is still scared from his behavior. From his threat.

"Bea?" Mel's head pops around the door.

"Hi, Mel," I say warmly. Mel is almost always at the Art Attic, pitching in wherever she's needed, but also lending thoughtful feedback and advice across all mediums. She's an artist through and through and working with her has been a wonderful experience.

"I'm glad I caught you." She enters the room, her eyes dancing over the pieces the class worked on today. Her fingertips dust across the edge of a bowl. "These are coming along beautifully."

"Yeah," I agree, glancing at the collection of pottery. "It's a wonderful group."

"They have a wonderful teacher."

I dip my head in thanks, blushing at her praise.

"I wanted to talk to you about the Inaugural Art Attic showcase in Knoxville." She beams. "It's our first one but I'm hoping it will be an annual occurrence."

I smile back. "That's great. When is it?"

"In five weeks."

"Oh, wow. That's soon. Do you need help with outreach? With spreading the word?"

"I absolutely do. Thank you."

"Of course."

"But I'm also hoping you'll contribute to the showcase. As one of our artists."

I freeze, my mouth falling open. Me? A contributing artist? "Really?"

Mel's expression softens, her eyes warm. Understanding. "Really. Your work speaks for itself."

"Thank you," I murmur. It's not that I don't think my pottery is good; I know it is. It's just that being valued as an artist, being recognized as a potter, is rare. Usually, people think of my pottery as a hobby, not a legitimate career path. But when I gain credentials, through showcases, when I gain a following, through networking, my prospects will change. This is a first step in that direction.

"Do you think you have time to do it?"

"Yes!" I say enthusiastically even though I'm going to have to work around the clock to make it happen. "I've been considering a few ideas for a while." That's the truth. I have a list of things I want to breathe life into...time has been the issue.

With this commitment, I'll have less time to see Cole. But Noelle DiSanto's words come back to me. *Don't give up your daydream for anyone.* Cole spends every second he can improving his game; why shouldn't I make the same commitment to my career?

"Excellent. If you want to talk through any ideas, I'd be happy to listen. To support however I can," Mel offers.

"Thank you. Truly, Mel, you have no idea what this opportunity means to me."

She smiles gently. "Yes, I do. I was in your shoes once. A long, long time ago." She chuckles. "I'm excited to see what you create, Bea."

"Thank you."

"I'll email you the details. Dates, location, the logistics." Mel stands from her chair. "See you tomorrow."

"See you!" I wave.

But the moment the door closes behind Mel, I get back to work. I pull out my notebook and pen and start outlining my ideas for the showcase. Tomorrow, I need to begin sculpting if I'm going to have the series completed in time.

There's no way I can let this opportunity slip through my fingers. A Knoxville Showcase a year after Nashville? This showcase can open doors to a future I've only dreamed of.

COLE

Miss you, B. Can I see you?

BEA

Just leaving studio.

COLE

Now? It's almost midnight.

BEA

Got news!

COLE

Come over and tell me?

I GRIN. More than anything, I want to head to Cole's. I want to climb into bed next to him, fall asleep in his arms, and wake up to his kiss.

BEA

Yes! Let me go home and check on Gran.

COLE

I'll meet you there. Drive back together.

BEA

You sure?

COLE

100%

BEA

See you in 15.

It's after midnight when I pull into Gran's driveway. Cole's car idles in front of the curb. I race to his window.

"There she is," he says, grabbing the back of my head and pulling my face through the window to kiss me hard. "Miss you so damn much."

A flicker of guilt flares in my chest. But Cole doesn't look upset, the way Jay used to, when I'd spend hours in the studio, thinking, experimenting, losing myself in the high that only sculpting provides. He just looks happy to see me. "Me too. Let me grab some things and check on Gran. I'll be out in a few."

"I'll be waiting."

"'Kay." I kiss him again before scurrying up the front porch and into Gran's house.

I tiptoe inside, skipping the creaky floorboard.

"Your father was better at this than you are," Gran's voice rings out.

I squeal, clenching my chest. "God, Gran, you scared the hell out of me."

"Don't take the Lord's name in vain."

I mush my lips together. Gran's a professional swearer but she never ventures into religion or anything that a believer would take offense to. I bow my head in apology.

"Is that your *beau*," she cackles, "in front of the house?"

"Yes. I just finished at the studio." I move closer to her rocking chair. "I wanted to check on you; I thought you'd be sleeping."

"I'm not an invalid, Beatrice."

"I know. I just, I wanted to kiss you good night." I kiss her temple.

Gran rolls her eyes. "Your father was a better liar too."

I laugh, knowing from countless stories, that my dad's courtship with my mom turned Gran prematurely grey. "I'm going to grab some things. If I sleep at Cole's, will you be okay?"

"I'll be fine knowing my granddaughter is out, a woman of the night, committing a series of sins."

I snort. "Hardly a woman of the night."

Gran grins, standing slowly from the rocker. "Have fun, Beatrice. You're only young once. Just, be careful." She turns a serious, solemn gaze on me.

"I am, Gran."

"Hope so, my girl. It's hard to mend a broken heart." With that, she hobbles slowly to her bedroom.

I watch her disappear around the corner. Does she think Cole and I don't stand a chance? Or was she hinting at Jay and his not coming around anymore? There's no love lost there; Gran and my brothers tolerated Jay, but they never liked him. I rub my wrists absentmindedly, wondering if they sensed the anger that simmered in his veins, concealed just below the surface. I hope Jay doesn't come around anymore.

I glance out the window, take in Cole's outline through the window of his car. He's waiting patiently, at twelve thirty in the morning, just so he can sleep next to me even though his alarm clock will go off in a handful of hours.

No, that type of dedication to making something work means we have a chance. We have a whole future ahead of us.

My mind made up, I turn and race up the stairs. I pack an overnight bag quickly. Then, I turn off the lights and lock the front door, bound down the porch steps, and slide into Cole's car.

"Ready?" He extends a hand to me as he pulls away from the curb.

I lace my fingers with his and squeeze. "All set."

FOURTEEN
COLE

"LOVE WAKING up with you in my bed," I tell Bea when she stirs to life, her cheek pressed into my chest. I kiss the top of her head, her curls tickling my nose.

I had an early morning run and got a stretch in outside before rinsing off and slipping back under the blankets with Bea. With her in my arms, my body unwinds, my mind clears, and I'm able to fully relax. It's a relief, not mentally crossing things off a check list or gearing up for the next item on the agenda.

For a handful of hours, usually when the rest of my town is sleeping, I revel in holding my girlfriend in my arms and just *be*. Be with *her*.

Bea turns her head, her lips dragging over my chest as she presses a kiss over my heart. "Me too." She sits up, wiping sleep from her eyes. "I can make pancakes for breakfast."

I grin. "You can but I have to pass. I had a smoothie."

She pouts. "You can't have one pancake?"

I shake my head, knowing I'm being strict but, "I'm in training."

"I thought you liked cupcakes?"

I snicker. "I love cupcakes. But one month of wooing you resulted in my eating seventeen cupcakes."

Bea laughs. "You counted?"

I shrug, knowing how strange it sounds to some people. "I track my nutrition. That month pushed me way off track."

Bea snuggles back beside me. "You sure you're not over-correcting?"

I kiss the crown of her head. "I'm sure."

"Okay. Well, I'll just have boring oatmeal."

I laugh, turning until I'm hovering over her. "I'll make it interesting for you," I say, kissing her neck. "I can add fruit." I move down to her chest, flicking my tongue over her nipple through her thin sleep tank. She sighs. "Almond butter," I mutter, my hand slipping up her shirt and smoothing along her ribs. "Flax seed."

"Less talking." Bea arches into me. "Oatmeal will never be sexy."

I snort, pulling her shirt up and over her head. "Fine. But you are, baby." Then, I kiss her hard and take my time showing her exactly how sexy I find her.

While Bea showers and I make her pancakes, my cousin Jamie calls.

"What's up, Jaim?" I answer.

"Dad and I are coming to Tennessee!" she squeals.

Excitement thrums through me. I miss my family, but I never put pressure on them to come for a visit, or catch a game, even though I offer to pay for the flights and tickets. My uncle would never accept a handout and I know it's hard for him to take off work. "When?"

"Next month! Your game against L.A."

"Really? I can't wait. I'll get you tickets. Hell, you can sit in the family box."

"Dad's buying—"

"Stop," I cut her off. "Listen, I get your dad wanting to do things his way, but coming to see me play means I get the good seats. For free. It's not a handout, it's freaking gratitude. I'd love for you to visit."

"I know," she agrees. "I'll talk to him."

"Family box. You're my family."

"Will your girlfriend be there?"

The water in the shower turns off and I smile. "Yes. I can't wait for you and Uncle Kirk to meet her. You're going to love her."

"I can't wait too. Even Dad's excited about it. I think he's a little shocked you have a serious girlfriend."

I chuckle, knowing she's right. My uncle constantly encouraged me to ask girls out, to have some fun, but I couldn't deviate from the plan. I had to get a scholarship, I had to play Division One, I had to get drafted. I needed to prove to everyone who thought I'd amount to nothing wrong. I needed to show them that I became a player in the NHL.

"Send me your dates; I'll sort out the flights."

"No way," Jamie says. "I may be able to convince Dad about the family box, but he'd never accept the flights."

I sigh. "I wish he'd accept a hell of a lot more. Everything I achieved is because of him, because of his and your support."

"You're sweet, Cole, but you would have made it no matter what. You're the most determined guy I know."

"I want your dad to take it easy," I say, not responding to her comment. My uncle and cousin think too much of me. Most of my drive comes from spite, but a tiny slice comes from wanting to live up to the man they think me to be. A hell of a lot more whole than I am.

"You and me both."

"Well, I can't wait to see you."

"Same. Block your social calendar while we're in town. I want to see Knoxville."

"What social calendar?" I ask.

"I don't know. Now that you've got a girlfriend, I imagine you're busy with, you know, plans and things?"

I chuckle. "Hardly. I'm at the arena all the time and Bea's working on a sculpting showcase. Pottery. She's everything, Jamie."

I can hear the smile in my cousin's reply. "I'm sure she is. But…" Her tone sobers. "Make sure you're making room for her in your life, Cole. You tend to have a one-track mind."

"We're good," I say, wanting to shut this conversation shift down. While I know Jamie's looking out, I don't need anyone's opinion or advice, no matter how well-intentioned it is, on my relationship with Bea. I ended it when Beau tried to interject, and I'll do the same with my family.

My relationship with Bea is between the two of us. If we understand each other, that's all that matters.

Jamie sighs. "Okay."

I soften my tone. "I'm really happy you're coming to see me."

"Me too." The smile is back. "Are you seeing Bea today?"

As if on cue, Bea enters the kitchen. Her hair is still damp, pulled into a high bun on top of her head, curls spilling out. "She just entered the kitchen. Gonna have some pancakes."

"You?" Jamie sputters. "Eat pancakes in the middle of training?"

I laugh. My cousin knows me well. "Gonna watch Bea eat," I amend.

Jamie snorts. "Go. Have a great breakfast. Tell Bea hello and I can't wait to meet her."

"Will do. Take care of yourself. If you need anything—"

"I'm fine, Cole."

"Call me."

"Goodbye."

"'Bye." I hang up the phone.

I grin at Bea who watches me closely. "Sit, I made you pancakes."

She wrinkles her nose. "You didn't have to do that."

"I wanted to," I tell her, placing down her dish and moving to fill her a mug with coffee and cream, one sugar.

I take the seat across from her. "My uncle and cousin are coming to visit. They're going to catch the L.A. game."

"Ooh, really?" Bea asks around a mouthful. "Damn, Cole. You're missing out. These are delicious."

I'd be lying if I said the pancakes, the maple syrup, weren't tempting. But I locked away my cravings years ago. My high school coach's voice rings in my mind whenever I start to cave. *If you want to be the best, you have to go all in.* "Thanks, babe. You enjoy them." I take a sip of water instead. "Jamie says hello and she can't wait to meet you."

Bea beams. "I'm excited to meet them too."

"Look at us, meeting the family."

"And all in the same month," she says, reminding me of Gran's party. "You're a relationship natural."

I laugh. "I think you make it easy."

Bea blows me a kiss and takes another bite of pancakes. "If you keep cooking like this, you'll never get rid of me."

"Then I need to up my game. Learn some new recipes."

Bea spears another bite of pancake with her fork. "Better get on that, Philips."

I lean over the table to take her hand. "Putting it on the top of my to-do list, Turner."

She grins. "Good."

I ADD another ten-pound plate to each end of the weight bar and slide underneath.

"You're gonna burn out," Damien Barnes comments.

"Nah." I shake my head, gripping the bar.

He swears and moves behind my head to spot me. Even though I don't need it, I'm too polite to tell him to back off.

"We already lifted this morning," he reminds me.

"You're here," I grit out as I bench press.

"I'm stretching." He snorts, his tone holding a thread of disbelief. "And making sure you don't suffocate if your arms give out."

I ignore him and complete my set, re-racking the bar. I sit up and mop the sweat off my face with the end of my tank. "My arms don't give out."

"You're getting cocky, Philips," Damien says it half as a joke, half as a warning.

"I'm not." I guzzle some water. "I'm just in training. I'm tracking everything, workouts, reps, calories, macros, everything. I know what I can handle, and I know when to pull back."

He watches me for a beat, his eyes more perceptive than most of the team gives him credit for. "If it becomes too much, you let someone know. You can call me."

"I know, man. Thanks. I appreciate you." I mean it too. Barnes is a decent guy; he's always looking out for the guys on the team. But I've always been this intense during training. I'm still trying to make up for the cupcake feast. I'm also trying to balance hockey with Bea. I need the workouts, the outlet they provide, the space to release my energy and calm my nerves.

"What's going on with you and Turner's sister?"

"Bea." I can't stop the grin that slides across my face at her name. "We're good. She's, she's the best."

Barnes smiles back. "Good. Happy for you, Rookie."

"Yeah, me too." I toss my water bottle into my gym bag. It feels good to be fulfilled, truly happy, for the first time in… maybe ever. "I'm taking off, Barnes. You good?"

He lifts a hand in farewell. "Just stretching, man. Catch you tomorrow."

"See ya." I head back to the locker room, take a quick shower, and head home.

I should be exhausted, after a run and two lifts, but my adrenaline is still high. Energy bounces around my body, restless and needing to be channeled into something productive. I text Bea.

COLE

Hey! You busy?

An hour passes with no response. Sighing, I force myself to go buy groceries, hoping she replies in the meantime. I'm looking up new dinner recipes when she texts back.

BEA

Hi! At studio.

COLE

Late night?

BEA

Another hour or so.

COLE

Hungry?

BEA

Always.

COLE

Come by? I'll make you dinner.

BEA

Beef Wellington?

COLE

(Laughing emoji) I learned my lesson. I scaled back. Pasta primavera.

BEA

I'll bring the wine.

COLE

Not drinking baby but I have wine for you. Just bring yourself.

BEA

Dessert?

COLE

If you want something special...

BEA

I guess I'll settle for you.

COLE

(Laughing emoji) Bring that sass too. I miss it. Miss you.

BEA

Same. See you soon.

I toss down my phone and set to work on dinner. I'm just finishing setting the table when Bea knocks on the front door.

"It's open," I call out.

She appears a moment later, her cheeks rosy, her hair messy, her shirt dirty. I smile. "You look beautiful."

"I look like a disaster."

"A beautiful one."

She snorts but comes into my open arms and kisses me. "It smells delicious."

"I'm putting in work, trying to keep you around."

Her eyes dance as she pulls away. "I'm not going anywhere, Cole."

"I hope not, babe." I smile when I say it, but the words come out heavy, filled with truth.

Bea's expression tempers and she leans up on her tippy toes, placing a sensual, soulful kiss to my mouth. Her lips roll over mine like a secret to share, and when I part my lips, she spills it into my mouth. I grip the back of her neck, kissing her with as much emotion as she's giving me.

Our kiss turns spicy, our chemistry igniting. I'm about to pick her up and relocate us to the bedroom when Bea pulls away. Her eyes hold mine. "Let's eat first," she says, her tone low. "I'm famished."

"Okay," I agree, my hand cupping her cheek. Then, I smile. "I'm better than dessert anyway."

"Much, much better."

We sit down and eat a delicious meal. It's normal and ordinary. It's something couples do all the time, it's something Bea and I have been doing for weeks. But tonight, something has shifted in the space between us. Our looks are more lingering. Our touches are more intentional.

I'm falling in love with this beautiful woman, and I don't want to give her up. I don't want to lose her. I never want to disappoint her. The thought of letting her down, of losing her, terrifies me.

When Bea scoops up her last penne and her plate is clean, I stand from the table and tug on her hand.

"The dishes—" She looks around the cluttered table.

"Can wait," I finish her sentence and pull her up. "I want you, Bea. Please."

Her eyes spark, desire and understanding washing over her expression. "Yes. Always, Cole."

She follows me into my bedroom and strips out of her dusty, dirty clothing. I lose my sweats and T-shirt. Tonight, when I take her into my arms, our connection is deeper. Our kisses last longer. Our coupling morphs into a lovemaking that is more meaningful than anything I ever experienced.

We orgasm together, coming down from our bliss in tandem. I pull back to look at her, to lose myself in her thundercloud eyes. "I love you, Bea."

A soft, sated smile crosses her face. "You have no idea all the things I feel for you, Cole." She leans up to kiss me. "I love you so much."

Emotions rock through me. They're sudden and intense,

creating a windstorm that rushes through my veins. I let the feelings sweep through me, grateful to experience them. Grateful to have the love of my life looking at me with wonder and love shining in her eyes. It's as undeniable as the love in mine.

I hold her close, kiss her softly. Again, our soft gives way to a steam that has us both reaching the highest pinnacle and tumbling down as one. Always together.

FIFTEEN
BEA

I RUN my fingers through my hair nervously. A ball of concern lodges in my throat. My to-do list is too long. My responsibilities stacking up until I feel like they're going to drag me under.

Two courses at the Art Attic.

My commitment, three nights this week, to Primrose.

Gran's caretaker. Her birthday party.

Planning the family dinner for my brother's arrival.

My showcase pieces, which mean the world to me.

The messages from high school friends I've been blowing off.

And Cole. Cole. Cole. Cole.

I haven't seen him all week and I miss him. I miss the way I feel when I'm with him—free and uninhibited. Present and swept up in a lightness that leaves me breathless and reeling and grateful.

I tap my fingers on the edge of the table, my third mug of coffee next to my hand. I'm jittery, anxious, and on edge, wondering how the hell I'm going to cram all the things I need to do in the teeny, tiny allotment of time I have until I need to head to The Honeycomb and sell cupcakes.

I blow out a deep breath.

CELINE

Hi, babe. I fly in the morning of the party. Sorry I can't come earlier but my schedule is bananas. Can I bring you anything from L.A.?

Shit! I need to tell Beau that Celine is attending Gran's party! I've been waiting for the right time to broach the subject, but considering there is no right time, I've been avoiding it.

BRODY

Blake and I land at 4 PM. Can you pick us up from the airport?

I gulp, fanning myself. Can I make that work? What am I supposed to do? Not greet my brothers at the airport when I haven't seen them in four months?

COLE

What do you call a fly with no wings?

I crack a smile. How can Cole distract me from the million things I need to focus on with a silly joke?

BEA

I'm stressing. But, what?

COLE

A walk.

COLE

Why stressing?

BEA

(Picture of my to-do list) (nervous face emoji)

My phone rings a second later.
I pick up. "Hi."

"Hey, baby. Are you at the studio?"

"Yes. I finished class and am trying to work on a piece for the showcase and then, I need to head to the arena. Except the caterer called about Gran's party, which, by the way, isn't a surprise but she doesn't know about all the family and friends flying in. I'm trying to coordinate my brothers' flights so I can do one run to the airport, but I think Bodhi gets in earlier than Brody and Blake. I—"

"Take a deep breath for me," Cole cuts me off, his tone soothing.

I frown.

"Do it," he laughs.

I pull in a breath, hold it for a beat, and release it in a whoosh.

"Again," Cole says.

I repeat the process.

"I'm looking at your to-do list."

"And?"

"And I think it's time to put your notice in at Primrose, babe."

I roll my lips together. "I've been thinking that too…"

"What's holding you back?"

I sigh. "Beau got me this gig to help me out."

"And it did help you out."

"Yeah, but leaving Noelle hanging feels ungrateful. Feels like I'm not looking out for Beau."

"Has Beau said that?"

"No."

"Is Noelle under the impression that you're looking for a more permanent placement within Primrose?"

I think back to Noelle's job offer and my bowing out of the option. "No."

"Okay," he says gently. "Babe, you can't take on guilt for making decisions about your career. About what's best for you to move forward. You're going to burn out if you keep trying to balance all these jobs and obligations."

"I know." I huff. "I'm also scared."

Silence ticks by. "Of?"

"I don't want to jinx myself."

"How is lightening your load jinxing yourself?"

I toss an arm out to the side even though I'm alone in the studio and no one can witness my exasperation. "You know, like I'm getting too cocky. Thinking too much of my ability to do this and—"

"You *can* do this."

"You don't know that."

"I do. Baby, I believe in you. But *you* need to believe in you if you're going to succeed. You need to know that you're making the right decisions to move forward. Burnout and feeling stressed and overwhelmed is just as much of a jinx as taking your shot."

"You're making too much sense, Cole," I lament the obvious.

He chuckles. "If you want this, you need to make decisions. Have a conversation with Noelle. Talk to your brother. I bet they both understand if you frame it the right way."

"I know." Deep down, I know he's right. If I wasn't spending three to four nights a week at The Honeycomb, I'd have that time to work on my showcase pieces. It would relieve a lot of the pressure I feel but making the decision to do it feels insurmountable.

Will Beau be angry? Will he think I'm making a mistake? In many ways, Beau raised me. He sacrificed for me. Even though he's my brother, I want his approval. Sometimes, it feels like I need it in order to be successful.

My phone buzzes with an incoming text.

BEAU

What time is family dinner before Gran's party?

I need to make the damn reservation!

"Bea?" Cole asks.

Shaking myself out of my thoughts, I focus on our conversation. "Sorry. My phone keeps buzzing with messages, reminders of things I need to do."

"I'll let you go."

"Okay. See you tonight?"

"Sorry, babe. I'm watching game-tape at Damien's tonight. Tomorrow?"

I close my eyes. "I'm putting in extra time at the studio."

"You need to decide how badly you want your pottery business."

"Yeah." Tears prick the corners of my eyes. Doesn't he realize how hard it is for me to make this decision?

Cole sighs. "Bea, is disappointing Beau also disappointing yourself?"

I let out a shaky breath and squeeze my eyes closed, overwhelmed. "It feels that way."

"Because Beau is your big brother?"

"Because he enlisted to help provide for my future," I admit quietly. While Beau enlisted for other reasons as well, my desire to attend art school was a big consideration. As a result, I never want to let him down. I never want him to think I'm not grateful for his sacrifice.

"A future he wants you to embrace, to be successful," Cole points out.

What if I give up a consistent gig and nothing comes of the showcase? Then I have to start the job-hunting process from scratch. *Don't give up your daydream for anyone.* Noelle DiSanto's words filter through my mind. I think Noelle will understand my desire to move on. But will Beau?

"Bea?"

Shit. "Sorry."

"Don't be. Do what you have to do. Hopefully I'll catch you after the game for a good night kiss."

"Yeah," I agree. "I'll see you tonight."

I hang up and stare at the piece in front of me. It's a huge centerpiece bowl I want to make the focal point of my showcase. It's intricate, with an ombre layering of natural colors. It requires my full focus, and my head is all over the place.

BODHI

Yo! Your boy, Jay, just hit me up for some ink. Something about your name??? Y'all back together? Think this through, Bea. He's NOT the one.

I drop my forehead to the edge of the table and groan. What the hell?

Why isn't Jay accepting my decision? Why is my family messaging me nonstop? Why doesn't anyone respect my time and understand I'm trying to create? To build something that means everything to me?

You need to believe in you.

I message Bodhi back.

BEA

DO NOT tattoo anything on Jay. Talk when I see you.

BODHI

You okay?

BEA

Yes. Miss you.

BODHI

We need to catch up, baby Bea. See you soon.

I heave out a sigh and clean up my workstation. Then, I head home to shower and change into my Primrose shirt. Before I leave Gran's, I leave a message for Noelle DiSanto.

Cole's right; it's time I start making some decisions about my future.

NOELLE WAS UNDERSTANDING and gracious about my two weeks' notice. Even though giving notice does nothing to alleviate my current commitments and intense schedule, if the showcase goes well, it will pay off in the future when I have more time to create.

But I have to deliver for the showcase first. It hangs over my head like a raincloud, this massive make it or break it moment that I want so badly, my fingers itch to reach out and take it. To make it happen.

Noelle understood my feelings exactly and offered to look at my business plan and give advice. I jumped at the chance and left for The Honeycomb feeling much more positive about the future.

During a lull in business, I wrote out a new to-do list, prioritizing the most pressing items. Between the bustle of cupcake-purchasers, the cheers for the Thunderbolts, the whir of thoughts in my mind, and the messy scrawl of notes I jot down, the game passes quickly.

I'm wiping down the counter when Cole wraps his arms around me from behind.

Squealing, I spin in his arms, my chest brushing against his. I grin, glancing up at my big, strong, solid hockey player. "How'd you play?"

He kisses me. "I did all right."

Barnes snorts, coming up beside us. "Rookie's being modest. He killed it."

Cole grins. It's boyish and pleased and lets me know just how happy he is to hear the praise. I slug him in the shoulder. "Holding out on me, Cole?"

He taps my ass lightly. "Never."

Beau appears, groaning. "Dude, don't fucking paw my sister in public."

Damien snickers as Cole wraps an arm around my shoulder and pulls me into his side.

I hide my face in Cole's side to conceal my laughter. Poor Beau isn't used to seeing me as an adult, as a woman, capable of making my own choices.

"You guys want to head to Corks?" Damien asks.

Cole glances at me, lifting an eyebrow. He doesn't want to press in case I have to beg off due to the stupid to-do list burning a hole in my pocket. My brother scowls at our non-verbal exchange.

I bite my bottom lip. Can I grab a drink and get in home in time to party plan?

Seeing my hesitancy, Cole makes a decision. Hugging me closer, he shoots a smile at Damien. "Not tonight, man. Bea and I are in full-on party planning."

Beau's eyes widen. "For Gran's birthday?"

I blush. "Yeah."

"I thought that was sorted," my clueless brother says.

I shake my head. "Not yet. Who do you think is planning it all?"

Remorse ripples over his face as he realizes just how busy I've been trying to put all the pieces together. "I can help."

Cole tips his head. "It's all right, man. I got it. You said you have plans tonight."

I've never seen Beau look so uncomfortable, out of his element before. He's usually the guy who swoops in to help me, but now, that role has been filled by Cole. His eyes flicker between Cole and me. Finally, he sighs. "Yeah, sure. You need me, Bea?"

"Nah," I say, relieved to be spending some much-needed time with my man. "Cole and I got it."

"Sure," Beau says, looking not sure at all.

Damien sighs. "You guys are really going to make me spend the night with Patton?"

I laugh. Cole grins. "See if you can rope Brawler into it. Maisy'll do you a solid."

"I have no idea how Maisy and Patton are such good friends," Damien mutters.

Cole shrugs. "Enjoy drinks."

Damien flips him off.

"You ready to get out of here?" Cole asks me.

"Yep." I lock up the pop-up stand. "All set." Reaching out, I squeeze my brother's forearm. The reminder that I need to talk to him about Celine, about Primrose, flits through my mind. But at the confused, almost lost look on his face, I hold back. "You good?"

"Yeah, Bea." He forces a smile that doesn't reach his eyes. Still shadowed, still haunted. "I'm good. Let me know if you need me."

I lean closer to kiss his cheek. "Love you, Beau."

He pulls me into a hug, holding on for longer than usual. "Love you too."

When Beau releases me, he lopes off. I glance over my shoulder, trying to figure out what's got him so twisted and down. I know it's been a tough transition for Beau, but lately, he's been more despondent than usual.

"Are you hungry?" Cole asks, taking my hand.

I turn away from Beau and look up at my boyfriend. "Starving."

"Same. I've got some chicken breasts I'm going to grill. You good with that or want to swing by a restaurant and grab takeout?"

I scrunch my nose. Boring chicken breast? I swear, Cole does not make any exceptions. I think all the Primrose cupcakes filled his sweets quota for eternity. Will he even have cake at Gran's party? I'm about to ask him when he adds, "Oh! I've got kale salad too."

Yay. "That works."

Cole squeezes my hand. "Perfect."

My sarcasm goes over his head, but I shake my head, silently laughing. Cole Philips is the most committed, dedicated man I know. Who am I to question his methods when it's clearly working for him?

SIXTEEN
COLE

"ARE YOU GETTING A BALLOON ARCH?" I ask Bea over chicken and kale.

At the last minute, I popped an organic flatbread pizza into the oven for her. The look of relief that crossed her face clued me in that she wasn't super impressed by the kale.

A bit of sauce dots the corner of her mouth as she scrunches her nose. "No. We're not balloon people."

I give her a look. "Who *isn't* a balloon person? What does that even mean?"

Slowly, she raises her hand. "I usually make the center-pieces and decorations."

I groan. "This is why you're overwhelmed."

"Because I like to add personal details to the parties I'm, by default, hosting?"

"Yes." I nod. "You need to delegate out. Besides, a luau needs balloons. It's in the party-planning bible."

Bea laughs and I'm glad I can elicit that reaction from her. Especially when I spoke to her earlier and she sounded on the verge of tears. I've heard that quivering before—Jamie gets it right before a meltdown. The thought of Bea caring so much, being concerned, about all the things on her plate that the plate would crack made me want to fix everything for her.

Hence, why I want to help her work through her list. She needs to prioritize and take decisions that will reduce the pressure she's under.

"I'm skeptical about the arch."

"That's because you've probably never posed under one," I toss back.

Her nose scrunches again as she wavers on how to let me down.

"Okay." I place my hand over hers. "Tell me your vision for this party. Then, we'll make a list—"

"Another list?"

I smirk. "For me. Whatever you feel comfortable handing off to me, I'll take care of."

Gratitude rings the edges of her irises. "Really?"

"Really." How hard can calling a couple vendors be? Balloons and flowers, done.

"Okay." She sits up straighter, her enthusiasm back. "I'm thinking we should stick with a pineapple theme. Nothing too on the nose, more natural and organic. Long, natural grasses—oh! Like pampas—and unbleached oak for the tables. We can alternate between benches and chairs for seating. Like rattan. Love that that's back in…"

Shit! As Bea describes her vision in detail—many, many details—panic begins to swim through me. What did I just agree to? What the hell is pampas? And rattan? And…what did she just say? A signature cocktail?

This birthday bash is important to Bea. It's more than the party. It's proving to her family, her brothers, herself, that she's capable of handling responsibility. That she can deliver on her promises. That she can…open a business. Excel in a creative field.

The pieces snap into place, offering clarity into the significance of this event. This event I just volunteered to support even though my plate is stacked too. I've got training and lifting. Running and practice. My meal prep alone is a full-time job. Not to mention the tracking. The meditation and visualization exercises to get into the mental headspace I need to perform on the ice.

Prove them all wrong.

My team is counting on me. My family is counting on me.

Hell, I'm counting on me. I need to prove that I can carry the future leadership of the Bolts. That I can contend for a top NHL team. That I have a future in this sport. At this level. Right now.

"Cole?"

I shake my head, snapping out of my thoughts when Bea says my name. "Huh?"

"You have no idea how much I appreciate your help. I still have two weeks at Primrose, although Noelle is trying to find my replacement sooner, so you're taking a lot off my plate." She slides a paper with a list—my list!—across the table. "Sometimes I wish I could just hire a party planner—"

"Can't you?" Why didn't I think of that? I'd gladly foot the bill if it would help Bea relax.

She shakes her head. "Gran really appreciates the little details." She shrugs. "I don't know, it feels like a cop-out to let someone else handle it entirely. So, thank you. Really."

Internally, I groan. Externally, I beam. "No problem, babe."

Except it is a huge fucking problem because I just invited a thousand distractions into my neat, orderly, routine way of life. I shove the list into my pocket.

"Do you want to come to the family dinner?" Bea asks. "It's just my brothers and Gran, the night before her birthday. My brothers are all flying in early to spend some time together so…it could be good to meet them all *not* at the party."

"Right." I force a chuckle. "Yeah, sure, I'd love to come." I mean it, too. I do want to meet Bea's brothers and spend some time with them. I want them to get to know me and trust me to be good to their sister. "Is Beau okay with it?"

Bea shrugs. "I don't see why not. We're dating."

I wrap my hand around Bea's wrist and squeeze. She flinches.

Frowning, I loosen my hold. "You okay?"

"Yeah," she laughs, averting my gaze. I drop my hand and she rubs at her wrist.

A wave of horror washes through me. "Bea? Did I hurt you?"

"What?" Her eyes widen, her mouth dropping open. "No, of course not." She rubs her wrist faster.

Something is off. Bea's never fidgety and right now, her eyes dart all over the kitchen and she rubs both wrists like she's going to break out in hives.

"What's going on?" I ask slowly, trying to sort out whatever the hell just transpired.

Tears spring to Bea's eyes and the emotion she shows causes my mind to clear and my body to lock down. Something fucking happened. "Are you sure I didn't hurt you? I didn't mean—"

"Jay came to the studio last month."

My eyes narrow, waiting.

"He..." She pauses, shaking her head. "I'm fine." She holds up a hand before I can rapid-fire questions at her. What the hell does that mean? What the fuck did he do? I zero in on her wrist. Did he fucking touch her? "He's having a hard time understanding that we're together."

"How hard of a fucking time?" I snap.

A tear slips down her cheek and I want to throw up. What the hell did he do to my girl? Could I have prevented it if I stood up for her earlier? Did she need my support in stopping him and I missed all the signs, assumed she handled it?

"It's nothing. He just grabbed me, that's all."

"That's not nothing," I shoot back, moving to her side of the table. I wrap her in a fierce hug, holding her close. "You're scared."

"He told me I'd regret it. Not getting back together."

I close my eyes, pressing my mouth to the crown of her head. My biggest fear tumbles from my mouth. "Do you?"

"What?" Bea pulls back, looking up at me with tears in her eyes. "Of course not."

"Bea," I whisper, pulling out the chair beside her and sitting down. "I'm sorry I didn't protect you."

"It's not your job."

"Of course it is." Visions from my childhood, handprints on my mom's cheeks, bruises around her throat, fill my mind. "Fuck!" I bring the butt of my fist down on the table. The plates jump and settle. Bea shrinks away from me and instantly, I feel fucking worse. "Baby, I'm sorry." How the hell could I lose my cool in front of her?

She reaches for me, her eyes burning with the same need I feel, and I wrap her back up in a hug.

"Why didn't you tell me?" I ask.

"I thought I handled it."

"Are you worried?" I murmur. I'm fucking worried. Worried and furious and—I should have put a stop to this shit. But I hate confrontation. I shy away from getting involved. My dad used his fists too much and by holding back, by not being like *him*, I put my girl at risk.

Bea shrugs.

Prove them all wrong.

"If he comes around again, promise you'll call me?"

She nods.

"I need the words, Bea."

"I promise. But I don't think he will."

"If he does—"

"I'll let you handle it."

"Good. Tell Beau too."

Bea makes a face.

"Why don't you want Beau to know?"

She blinks rapidly. "I want to prove to him that I'm an adult. That I can make decisions about my future." Her voice pitches lower. "That he can trust my judgement."

"I get that, baby. But your safety is non-negotiable. You have a lot of people that care about you. Let us in. Let us help. Please." My voice cracks.

She holds my gaze but slowly nods. "Okay. I will."

I take a deep, cleansing breath. "What do you need, baby?"

She scurries into my lap, clinging to me. "Just you."

My arms wrap around her waist, pinning her to my chest. I kiss her hard.

Being close to Bea centers me. I need her just as badly as she needs me.

After an intense kiss, Bea pulls back and rests her head on my shoulder. I stroke my fingers through her hair, down her back, and back up again. "The thing with Jay rattled me on top of everything else."

"I'm sorry that happened."

"I'm more worried about getting everything done on time."

"I got you, baby." Bea's never been anything but present for me and the one time she asks me to step up, well, I *offer* to step up, I need to show her it's a two-way street. That I support her too. "Let me handle Jay. We'll finish your list. And I'll be at the dinner."

Bea presses a kiss to the side of my neck, relaxing in my arms.

I tighten my hold, hopped up on adrenaline and regret and fear.

My mind races and my body feels jittery because…how the hell am I going to pull this off?

OTHER THAN A HANDFUL of text messages—no sign of Jay, Bodhi arrived—I haven't spoken to Bea all day. While I got a run in this morning, I'm behind on my lift. I still have a handful of things to cross off the to-do list for Gran's party. And I'm supposed to attend her family dinner tonight.

I glance at my Apple Watch and swear. I need to decide. I'll have to skip some of the list items to attend tonight's dinner. Or miss this dinner but have everything done for the party tomorrow.

Fuck. Either way, I'm letting Bea down. Guilt and failure line my stomach and I feel nauseous. Why the hell did I agree to this? Why didn't I realize it would be too much?

This is why I don't do distractions. When you let people in, there are expectations you're obligated to fulfill. Right now, I'm letting my girlfriend down and I fucking hate it.

I dial Jamie.

"Hey!" my cousin answers.

"If you were dating someone—"

"Uh-oh."

"And you had to let him down—"

"Shit. What happened?"

"Would you prefer he bailed on a family dinner—"

Massive gasp.

"Or skipped some items on a birthday bash to-do list you promised to fulfill for his grandmother's party?"

"You're screwed."

"Fuck," I swear. "Tell me about it." Ever since I learned about the shit Jay pulled, coupled with this to-do list, I've been reeling. My head is all over the place and my body feels ready to snap.

"When's the party?" Jamie asks.

"Tomorrow."

She groans. "How many people?"

"Seventy. Seventy-five."

"Damn!"

"Gran's a popular lady. And it's her ninetieth."

"I'll say. I hope I *know* that many people in my seventies."

I snort. "Same. What do you think I should do?"

Jamie sighs. "What's more important to Bea—the party or the dinner?"

I think about the pressure Bea's been under. About how she's taken on this party-planning role and run with it, clearly trying to prove something to her family. Or to herself. "I *think* the party. She's been really stressed about it and all her brothers, except for Beau, are flying in to attend."

Jamie's quiet for a beat. "Okay, I say skip the dinner. At least if the party stuff is done, she won't lose face in front of her family and friends. And you can explain that completing the list took longer than you thought and you didn't want to disappoint her or go back on your word. Even though you're super sorry about the dinner."

"Right," I say, breathing a sigh of relief. When Jamie words it that way, it sounds like I'm doing the right thing. Making the right decision. I don't bother mentioning my lift because Jamie will tell me to skip it, but...I can't. Missing one lift will lead to skipping a run. I was planning to have some cake and drinks at the party, but if I don't workout, will I enjoy myself at the event? Besides, with all the stress coiling in my body, I need the release a workout provides. I need to sweat this shit out.

"Cole," Jamie says slowly. "You're overthinking this. Text Bea and tell her you're working on the party stuff, and you want it to be perfect. You're super sorry but you can't make dinner. Then, offer to go to the party early and help her set up."

"Okay, okay." That's a good plan, isn't it? I'm messing shit up but not all the way. Not too badly. Right?

"Go. Message her!"

"Okay. Thanks, Jaim."

"Talk to you later."

I end the call and clench my phone.

Putting this in a text feels shitty so I call Bea. It rings several times before her voicemail picks up. Damn.

I'm texting her when a message comes through.

BEA

Hey! Sorry, can't chat. Just leaving to pick up
the twins from the airport with Bodhi.
What's up?

I cringe. Bodhi's first impression of me is going to be my bailing on dinner.

Sighing, I tap out the message.

COLE

Babe, I'm so sorry. This list took longer than I
thought. I swear I'll have it all done in time
tomorrow, but I can't make dinner tonight.

I press send and grip the phone.

Minutes pass without a reply and I feel like throwing up. Why didn't I manage my time better? Why did I take on too much? Why does letting Bea down feel like the worst thing in the world? Worse than losing a game or taking a jab to the face?

BEA

I understand. I'm sorry the list was so much.

Shit. Now, she feels guilty.

COLE

Not at all. I just didn't manage my time well.

I bite my inner cheek.

COLE

I'll come early tomorrow, help you set up.

BEA

No pressure.

I roll my eyes.

BEA

Come whenever.

COLE

Have fun tonight with your brothers. I'll see you tomorrow, babe. I love you.

Please say it back. Please.

BEA

Love you too. Thanks for your help, Cole.
Really.

I let out a slow exhale at her message. Even though I know she's not mad, I still feel awful.

I still feel like a failure.

Shouldering my gym bag, I head to the arena and lift until my arms give out.

SEVENTEEN
BEA

"TROUBLE IN PARADISE?" Bodhi asks on the way to the airport.

I shoot him a smirk before turning back to the road. I really wanted Cole to meet my brothers before Gran's party. Tomorrow is going to be chaotic, with so many friends and family in town, and I want the focus on Gran. Not me and who I'm dating.

Since I haven't introduced my family to anyone since Jay—and that was almost by default—a guy meeting my brothers is a big deal. I want them to have time to talk and get to know each other. Not a quick greeting as my brothers are all pulled into other conversations with friends who haven't seen them in forever.

"Beau says you're dating his teammate," Bodhi adds.

"You'll like Cole," I promise.

"I haven't met him yet so no opinion either way."

I roll my eyes.

Bodhi rests his elbow on the center console, his ink on full display. "What's going on, baby Bea?" He calls me my childhood nickname and for the strangest reason, tears prick the corners of my eyes.

Bodhi and I have always been close; he's always the brother I turn to when I need advice. There's so much sitting on the tip of my tongue, so many things I want to confide in him, but I don't know how to start without it all spilling out.

I'm not sure if I'm ready for it all to spill out. Will he think leaving Primrose was the right decision? I still haven't told Beau—about Primrose or Celine's visit. Should I start with the courses at the Art Attic? Confide in him about the showcase? Right now, only Cole and my college roommate know I've been asked.

Or do I tell him about Jay and how Cole's been on edge since my confession earlier this week? Emotionally, I'm rattled. I'm disappointed Cole isn't coming tonight. It's stupid though, he's not coming to *help* me. I'm the one who delegated a bunch of tasks his way since I'm the one struggling.

"Bea?" Bodhi leans closer, concern heavy in his tone.

I shoot him another smile that falls flat. "I'm fine, really. Just, a lot going on."

"Is caring for Gran too much? Do you need support?" The kindness in his tone almost breaks me. I hate myself for being weak, for wanting to break down.

My brothers have given me an amazing life considering I was orphaned at nine. It's my turn to step up for them and I'm—what?—buckling under the pressure of having a shot at my dream career with my dream guy?

"No," I say quickly, shaking my head. "Being home with Gran has been fine. Nice even," I add, thinking about our lunches and dinners. "She's in a good place and I love spending time with her. I'm happy you're all here so we can celebrate her together tomorrow."

Bodhi touches my elbow and I give him a quick look before merging onto the highway. "You know you can talk to me, right?"

"I know."

"Is Jay giving you a hard time? About the new guy?"

I sigh. "Jay hasn't been around in a while." It's technically true. Jay hasn't appeared on Gran's porch or at the Art Attic. But he has sent me a few texts. Telling me he's sorry for how he handled himself. That he misses me. That he'll never stop loving me. "But yeah, that's part of it."

Bodhi, misreading the severity of my statement, smirks. "Cole probably can't stand him either."

My throat tightens and I bite my lip. No one in my family liked me with Jay. It's one of the reasons Beau and Bodhi encouraged me to apply to art schools outside of Knoxville. Silence descends between us as I process my thoughts and search for the words I want to share.

I open my mouth to tell Bodhi about what transpired with Jay. Maybe after that, I'll tell him about the showcase. I'll ask him to read my business plan. "Bodhi, I—" His phone rings and I clamp my lips together.

"Sorry, I gotta take this." Bodhi answers the call. "Hey man, I'm glad you reached out."

Bodhi spends the rest of the ride discussing a huge back piece with an important client. I can tell by the tone of his voice that his client is big-time and Bodhi wants to impress him. My brother is doing big things, inking professional athletes and popular musicians, sponsoring concerts at huge venues. He even made an appearance on a reality TV show. Bodhi's the most natural resource for me to tap into.

I hesitated. I didn't dive into the conversation when he gave me the opening to do so.

I bite my tongue until it hurts and blink back tears.

Why can't I get it together? Why can't anyone see that I'm desperate for more?

You need to believe in you.

Cole was right. More than anything, I wish he was here with me. He would know I'm struggling. He wouldn't have taken the call but waited me out.

For years, I've tried to show my brothers that I'm a

capable adult. That I can make sound decisions. I want them to be proud of me, to know that their sacrifices weren't in vain.

But I'm floundering and it hurts. It also hurts that Cole isn't here.

I pull into the airport parking and ease into a spot. Taking a deep breath, I remind myself that tonight's dinner is one I've been looking forward to since we were last all together, four months ago. I'm not going to ruin it with anything dramatic or negative. Instead, I'll hug my brothers, listen to their exciting lives, and be as supportive as possible.

The caring, doting, loving sister. The way I always am.

"WAIT, YOU'RE LAUNCHING A NEW BUSINESS?" Beau asks Brody over dinner.

Brody nods, finishing his bite of steak. "Yeah." He points the tines of his fork toward Blake. "We're still getting investors."

"The tech part is pretty straightforward. It's the legal jargon that's taking forever." Blake grins, taking a swig of his beer.

As the twins discuss their new venture, something to do with healthcare tracking, I try to think of an intelligent question to ask.

Beau rattles them off. Bodhi asks logical business questions. And I take it all in, my brothers in all their glory, feeling worse than I did in the car.

"What's going on with you, baby Bea?" Brody asks as the server passes out dessert menus.

I open my mouth to tell him about the Art Attic, but Beau beats me to it. Pushing gently against my shoulder, he says, "She's dating my teammate."

"What?" Blake laughs, his eyes flashing. "Since when?"

"Do we like this teammate?" Brody asks.

"He's a good guy," Beau admits, begrudgingly. "Cares about Bea."

"He treating you right?" Blake looks at me.

I nod, taking a sip of my Coke. "You'll meet him tomorrow. Cole is—"

"Nothing like Jay, I hope?" Brody cuts in. I roll my eyes.

"Yo, I knew I forgot to tell you something, Beau. Jay tried to hit me up for ink," Bodhi tosses out, shaking his head. "Imagine, he wants to tat Bea's name, or a bumblebee or some shit, on his pec. And baby Bea's got a new man."

My brothers laugh and I feel my face heat, embarrassed but also *hurt*. Jay is a stressor hanging over my head. Cole is important to me. I want my brothers to take my relationship seriously, to recognize that I'm growing up and starting a new chapter in my life.

Instead, I order a slice of cheesecake and dull my fiery emotions in sugar and butter.

"MORNING, BUTTERCUP." Cole palms my ass as he comes up beside me.

I turn and smile, nestling into his side for a hug.

I stayed up late last night, restless. Sleep eluded me for hours as my mind churned. Why didn't I tell my brothers about the showcase? Why didn't I ask Bodhi for business advice? Why was I frustrated with Cole for not showing up when I knew he had a valid reason?

The whole ordeal left me reeling, feeling guilty and immature. Two things I despise.

"You good?" Cole keeps his arm wrapped around me as he kisses my temple.

I nod into his shirt, breathing in his cologne and holding it in my lungs.

"How was dinner?"

"Okay," I say slowly, wondering how much to reveal. Is now the best time to talk about my brothers? We're supposed to set up for Gran's party. Bodhi took her out for lunch so she wouldn't comment on the decorations. Or notice the friends and family arriving early to surprise her.

She has no idea two of her friends are coming into town. The three of them lived together on base when Grandpa served. It's been years since she saw them and now, they're all widows craving a reunion. I know their presence is the best gift we could give her besides our family attending. My cousins are arriving this morning along with aunts and uncles.

"What happened?" Cole pulls away, a frown etched between his eyebrows. "I swear to God, if Jay—"

"I didn't tell my brothers about the showcase."

Cole's frown deepens. "Why not?"

I shrug, turning away and fiddling with a paper lantern. "What if I'm rushing into it? What if they're not supportive? What if the showcase doesn't go well? And"—I throw an arm out toward him—"isn't it enough that they're meeting you today?"

Cole's eyes study me, perceptive as hell. "You're disappointed I didn't come to dinner."

I sigh, my guilt escalating. I close my eyes. "I have no right to be."

"But you wished I was there."

"I wished you were there," I admit.

Cole hugs me close again. "I'm sorry, Bea."

"Don't be. You were helping me. You were helping for this party." I glance over at the pampas grass he brought.

He's quiet for a long moment. "And I had a lift."

"A lift?" I turn back to him.

He nods, his cheeks red. "I can't get off track," he says it like an apology. "I can't lose hockey. Or you."

"You're not going to lose either." I face him fully, trying to understand his expression. His concern.

He gives me a soft smile and pulls me into his arms again. Cradling me against his chest, he kisses me. "I love you, baby."

"I love you too," I reply, trying to grasp the subtext of our conversation.

An hour ago, I thought I was reeling; now I feel even more stressed. Cole's here, helping me, showing up for me and yet...he couldn't skip one extra lift? I frown as I study him, trying to understand if his motivation and dedication runs deeper than his commitment to the Bolts. *Why* is he so hell-bent on working out several times a day? He'd still be an incredible player if he missed a workout or a run once in a while...

"Can I help you set up? What's our time frame?" Cole asks.

I heave out a breath and switch my attention to the party. Right now, Gran is my main priority. This party and being with my brothers and visiting with my family. Afterwards, I can figure out the nuances between Cole and me. I can worry about the showcase. I can make a new to-do list.

EIGHTEEN
COLE

DELIGHT WASHES over Gran's face as she takes in the scene before her. Bea's brother, I'm assuming Bodhi by all the ink on his arms and neck, stands beside her, helping her walk into the yard. Her friends and family gather, calling out greetings and birthday wishes as she steps into their warm embraces.

Bea looks over at me, tears in her eyes. "Thank you," she mouths.

I blow her a kiss, humbled by her emotion. By her gratitude.

"Happy birthday, Gran." Bea steps closer to her grandmother, wrapping her in a hug as Gran grips her shoulders, clearly overwhelmed by the amount of people in her yard.

The decorations look beautiful. Long, oak tables are set up with benches on both sides. Clusters of rattan-style chairs dot the yard, the small tables set with charcuterie boards and pickings. Pineapple and floral centerpieces burst with color. Tiny paper lanterns, interspersed with strands of light for when dusk settles, decorate the space.

It's understated but elegant, filled with warmth and love

and gratitude for the woman who celebrates ninety trips around the sun.

"Hey, man." A guy steps beside me.

I smile, holding out a hand. "You must be Brody or Blake."

He smirks. "Brody."

"Good to meet you. I'm Cole."

Brody sizes me up for a minute before shaking my hand. "Nice to meet you too. How long you been dating Bea?"

I hide my smile at his attempt to feel me out. I'm sure he knows all the details from Beau but the fact that he cares enough to ask, that he wants to know more about the guy dating Bea, makes me like him more. Bea deserves brothers who support her, who care about her happiness and help her achieve it. "A few months," I respond, glancing at Bea in the center of a huddle of cousins and aunts. "And I'm crazy about her."

Brody chuckles. "That's always good to hear."

"Yeah, we…" My words trail off as a fucker I never want to see again stumbles into the backyard. "Excuse me, Brody." My voice is clipped, my tone lethal. My hands clench into fists as a rage, the same type that used to grip my father, the one that scared me as a kid, swells to life.

Brody frowns, startled. Then, he follows my line of vision and swears. "Listen, man, Jay isn't—"

"He put his hands on her," I cut him off, knowing Bea didn't tell her brothers. If she did, one of them would have tackled him by now.

"What?" Brody hisses.

"Grabbed her wrists, threatened her. It's been months and he's still hassling her." I narrow my eyes at him. "She say anything to you?"

Brody's mouth twists, horror filling his eyes. "Nothing."

"Yeah, well, I don't think I know the full extent of it either."

"Fuck. He fucking asked Bodhi to tattoo her name and—"

I stalk away from Brody, heading toward the piece of shit who scared my girl.

Bea appears in my peripheral vision, her hair wild, her eyes panicked. "Cole—"

"Go out front," I demand Jay. Looking at Bea, I hiss, "Not trying to make a scene, baby. But he shouldn't fucking be here."

Bea closes her eyes, her expression pained.

I'm sure she doesn't want anything to ruin Gran's party. But there's no way in hell I'm going to sit back and let Jay stare at her, make her uncomfortable, in her home either.

Jay glares at me but shuffles toward the front of the house. He's swaying on his feet, his movements erratic. Fucking hell.

"Cole—" Beau appears at my side. Anger lines his face. "This isn't the time or—"

"You know he put his hands on her?" Brody interjects.

Bodhi's neck snaps up.

Tears swim in Bea's eyes.

I give her one long, apologetic look. "I love you, Bea. I love you so damn much I won't stand back while *anyone* hurts you."

One of Bea's cousins claps her hands and loudly tells the story of Gran and her two Army wives' friends. She draws most of the attention to a back corner of the yard and I'm supremely grateful. While Gran looks worried, she's quickly pulled into conversation with her friends and family.

I cut to the front of the house, with Bea and her brothers on my heels.

Jay turns as soon as I reach the porch and swings at me. His aim is wild, his eyes glazed. Fuck, I know that look. He's on something. Drugged up and too stupid to realize the mistake he's making. One hit and I can take him down.

Instead, I catch his fist and bend his arm, bringing him to his knees. A painful cry cracks through the air.

Bea whimpers but I don't turn around. Her brothers step up, but Beau shakes his head, letting me handle this.

The way I should have from the beginning.

Prove them all wrong.

Instead of letting my fists fly, the way I desperately want to, I take a measured approach. "You're fucked up," I tell Jay, kicking him over. When he's flat on his back, I plant my heavy shoe in the center of his abdomen.

He wheezes out a breath, his eyes half closed. Blowing out a sigh, I remove my foot and sit next to him. Reaching out, I pull him up by his shirt. He slumps over. "You're hurting." I shake him a little. "I get it; I fucking do. I'd wanna obliterate myself if I lost her too."

In my peripheral vision, I see the tears that coat Bea's cheeks.

"Fuck," Bodhi mutters, wrapping an arm around his sister.

"You need help, man. You need serious help and I'm going to make sure you get it," I say. Slowly, Jay's eyes roll to mine. "But don't mistake my kindness for weakness. You will never put your hands on Bea, or any woman, again. Or I'll fucking end you," I say through clenched teeth, seething with anger. With resentment. How many times did I sit beside my strung-out father? How many times did I witness him hurt my mom?

How many times did I feel the sharp pain of his fist?

But I am not my father; I'm so much fucking better.

Prove them all wrong.

"Do you understand me?" I snap.

Jay half nods, half slumps.

Beau steps forward and hauls him up by the back of his shirt. "Get him some water," he tells Blake.

As Blake enters the house, Bodhi makes a call. "His brother will be here in ten."

I nod, stepping away from the porch. Bea rushes me,

winding her arms around my waist and crying into the front of my shirt. "Shh," I mutter, stroking her back. "You're okay, babe. I got you."

"I know," she whispers into my shirt. "I love you, Cole."

I hold her tighter. I note the flicker of approval in Brody's eyes. I see the acceptance in Bodhi's stance. I feel the respect in Beau's hand on my shoulder. "Thanks for looking out for her."

"Always," I tell her brothers. "I'll always look out for her."

"What's going on? Bea, are you okay?" a panicked voice rings out.

We all turn toward the sound of heels clicking on the pavement. My mouth drops open. "You're Celine Hernandez." The famous Hollywood actress. I knew Bea had a friend, a sister-type relationship, with a woman named Celine but—the ultra-famous Hollywood star? Bea pulls back. "You've been holding out on me, babe."

She chuckles, her cheeks stained in tears, her eyes lined with love. Bea turns toward Celine, her arms open to pull her into a hug. But Beau steps in front of her, blocking her path to her friend.

"What the hell are you doing here?" Beau bites out.

Bodhi's eyes ping pong between them.

Blake returns with a water glass he shoves at Jay while staring, his mouth open, at Beau and Celine.

"Shit," Brody mutters.

"Hi, Beau," Celine says, her sultry voice causing Beau to flinch. "It's been a long time."

I work a swallow, my arm snaking around Bea's waist.

And then, the tension increases tenfold.

NINETEEN
BEA

"WHY DIDN'T you tell me about Jay?" Bodhi hisses at me.

I shrug, lifting a hand in farewell as Jay's brother loads him into the back seat of his car and takes off. He promised he'd talk to his dad and get Jay into rehab. I had no idea Jay was struggling so badly. I'm grateful Cole caught the signs and got Jay help instead of pummeling him the way I thought he would. But the fact that Cole knows enough to recognize the signs breaks my heart. It offers a glimpse into Cole's childhood that he usually glosses over.

I lean my head back against Cole's strong chest. His arms wrap around my waist, one hand splaying over my stomach. Cole kisses my temple. "You okay?"

I tip my head up. "Are you?"

His hold on me tightens. "I am now."

I place my hand on top of his and squeeze. "Thank you, Cole."

He squeezes back in response.

"You should have told me," Bodhi continues.

"I thought I had it handled," I say, shrugging.

My brother shakes his head, guilt rimming his eyes. Then he looks to the corner of the front yard where Beau and Celine are talking for the first time in eight years. "You think they'll be okay?"

I study Beau's shuttered gaze, the tension in his shoulders. Celine's arms are crossed over her chest, defensive and protective. I sigh. "I don't know. I hope so."

"Me too," Blake mumbles, standing from the porch step. "He'll never meet a woman like Celine."

"And no one will love her like Beau," Brody adds.

"How long did they date?" Cole wonders, putting the pieces of their epic love story together.

"All through middle and high school," I say. "They broke up when Beau enlisted, and Celine moved to L.A."

"Or Celine moved and Beau enlisted," Bodhi offers. "We're still confused as to which choice spurred the other's decision."

"Ah," Cole mutters.

"Well," Gran says, shuffling into the front yard. "This is some party."

Cole's chest rumbles with laughter beneath my head.

"I look around and the whole Turner clan is gone, wreaking havoc in the *front* yard. Where anyone can see," Gran continues, moving closer to me.

"Good thing we live in the country," I remind her.

Her eyes narrow but I spot the humor in them. "Pay per view," we say in unison, laughing.

I push off the wall of muscle behind me and open my arms. Gran comes into them and squeezes me. "Thank you for my party, Beatrice. I know it was all you."

"Cole helped," I admit.

Gran's eyes soften. "Of course he did."

"I love you, Gran."

"I love you, too. Even if you bring too many boys to the front porch."

We laugh together.

"Celine!" Gran calls out, interrupting Celine and Beau's

exchange. Gran cuts Beau a warning look. She holds out a hand to Celine. "Come talk to me. Beau hasn't earned back the right to hog your attention." She turns back to the yard. "Yet," she calls over her shoulder.

"Damn," Cole whispers. "She's fierce."

"A lioness," I say proudly, watching my ninety-year-old Gran be the life of her party.

"I see where you get it from," Cole says.

I don't know if it's the sincerity in Cole's voice or the strength Gran demonstrated or the fact that my whole family is here, in one place. But I open my mouth and at the most inopportune time, with the shadow of Jay still lingering on the porch and hurt blazing in Beau's eyes as Celine walks away from him, I make an announcement. "Family!"

My brothers freeze, staring at me.

Cole's hand reaches for mine, squeezing the last bit of encouragement I need to believe in myself.

"I have a showcase in two weeks. It's in Knoxville and it's a pretty big deal. I'd love it if you can come."

A grin splits Bodhi's face. Pride shines in Brody's eyes. Blake lets out a surprised laugh. Beau pulls up short, staring at me like he's seeing me for the first time.

"Of course I'll be there, baby Bea," Bodhi says.

Brody and Blake exchange a look. "We'd love to come," Blake says. "We'll just stick around an extra two weeks."

I widen my eyes.

"We've got some business meetings we can line up on the East Coast," Brody explains.

Beau holds out his arms and Cole drops my hand. I rush my eldest brother, wrapping my arms around him. "I'm sorry I didn't tell you about Celine."

"I'm sorry you felt like you couldn't tell me about Primrose and this showcase," he replies, regret in his tone.

"Noelle spilled the beans?"

Beau snorts. "You mean after she found your replacement? Yeah."

I kiss his cheek. "I love you, Beau. But I'm all grown up now."

Beau heaves out a tremendous sigh, as if he's carrying the weight of the world. I'm sure most of the time, it feels that way. "I know, Bea. And I'm so fucking proud of you."

"We all are," Bodhi chimes in, tossing an arm around my and Beau's necks. Brody and Blake step into the huddle, hugging and squeezing the hell out of me.

Bodhi laughs, glancing at Cole. "Get in here, big guy. We can tell you'll be sticking around."

Cole laughs but joins in on the family hug. I close my eyes and soak it all up.

THE FOLLOWING ten days pass in a blur. I throw myself into my work at the studio. Cole is the most focused I've ever seen him as the play-offs loom and the pressure on the Bolts to qualify picks up.

A few days before my showcase, Bodhi rolls back into town. Gran's excited to have us all under her roof as even Beau decides to spend the weekend sleeping at the house.

Early in the morning, while Beau, Brody, and Blake snore, Bodhi and I are up early, just like old times.

"Want to get breakfast?" he asks.

"Diner," I confirm.

We grin at each other—old memories of a past life flickering between us. Early morning diner breakfasts were a norm back when Dad would take Beau and the twins to the ice rink and Mom would treat Bodhi and me to breakfast.

On the way to the diner, I text Cole. He messages back that he just wrapped up a run and is heading to the gym for a lift.

I sigh, worrying that he's pushing himself too hard. I know his next few games are intense, but is there more to Cole's training? Am I missing something? As usual, he assures me this is par for the course. That he has everything under control and knows his limits.

I don't want him to worry about my growing concerns, so I back off. As soon as the showcase is over and the Bolts know if they qualified for the play-offs, we'll talk.

"You okay?" Bodhi asks as I slide into the booth across from him.

"Yeah. Cole's just pushing himself really hard. I worry."

"Can't cut it at his level without pushing."

"I know." I pick up a menu, hoping this breakfast distracts me from Cole and his commitment to hockey.

"Man." Bodhi grins. "I miss this place."

I glance around the old timey diner. "Me too," I say, nostalgia hitting me. "It's been a long time."

"Bea," my brother captures my attention. "Why didn't you tell me how serious you are about starting a business? I could help you."

I heave out a sigh. "I know." I pull my business plan, currently a stack of papers with haphazard notes and unfinished thoughts, out of my bag and slide it across the table. "I'd like your help. I know this is a mess, and I've already received awesome feedback from Noelle DiSanto. I still need to implement her thoughts but...it's a work in progress."

"Nah." Bodhi shakes his head and grasps the stack. "I wrote my first business plan on a napkin."

I smile. Bodhi and I order pancakes and coffee for breakfast before diving into my plan.

"What's your top goal?" he asks.

"I want to have my own shop."

"Can you do that on your own or do you need investors?"

I shake my head at the sly grin crossing his face. "I don't want your money."

"Come on, baby Bea. You know we'll all support you—whatever way you need—to make this happen. And if you don't know that, then I want to show you how serious I am. I'll front you cash."

"Nope." I shake my head. "I'm doing this my way."

At the steel in my tone, Bodhi snorts out a laugh. I know he's surprised that I turned his generous offer down, since I've always accepted Bodhi's advice and support in the past, but the hint of respect in his eyes solidifies my decision. I'm doing this my way. I believe in it.

"Okay. How do you get investors?"

"Who aren't my brothers?" I arch an eyebrow.

Bodhi chuckles but nods.

"Well, the showcase is important for networking. There's a chance I could connect with someone there. Ideally, I'd have completed a prestigious program, like the Landry Artistic Achievement program, that serves as a feeder into the art world. Investors, clients, mentors, the whole thing."

"How do you do the program?" Bodhi thanks our server for the coffee.

I fix mine the way I like it and stir it up. I snort. "It's a long shot. If you're not legacy, or don't have a connection—"

"Izzy's mom?" Bodhi cuts in, referencing my college roommate.

"Nah, she used her pull for Izzy and Iz wasn't accepted."

"Damn," Bodhi whistles, taking a sip of his coffee.

"It's big-time. But that's another route. Other than that, just word of mouth. Slowly building relationships, doing art shows around town and within the state." I shrug. "Build from the ground up."

"And this is what you want to do?" Bodhi's eyes don't waver from mine, but I catch the thread of skepticism in his tone.

"You built a booming business from the back of a van," I remind him.

"Yeah," he agrees. "But I wouldn't wish that on you, baby Bea."

"Maybe you should." I tilt my head. "I want to prove myself, Bodhi."

"To whom?" His eyes narrow.

"Everyone," I admit. "But mostly to myself."

Bodhi sighs but understanding rounds out his features. "Okay, Bea. I hear you. Let's get to work."

Our pancakes arrive and I cut into mine with a renewed sense of hope. I may not have planned to move back home, but now, I'm happy I did. I met the love of my life. I'm chasing the dream of my heart. I've earned the respect of my brothers. It didn't happen overnight and, like my business plan, it's a work in progress. But I'm proud of the moves I'm making. I'm happy exactly where I am.

Bodhi and I spend two hours poring over my notes and turning the scribbles, along with Noelle's advice, into a respectable business plan. When I get home, I text Cole.

BEA

Business plan done! I'm heading to the studio to finish a piece for the showcase.

COLE

Great job, Bea!

BEA

What are you up to?

COLE

Meeting with Coach and then meal prep. See you later?

BEA

Yeah, I'll message you when I get home.

COLE

Talk later.

I try not to read into his abrupt text messages. Usually, he'll send me a joke or elaborate. Today, he's direct, almost abrupt. I know he's been focusing more on his workouts, his nutrition, his play on the ice. The bead of worry I felt this morning expands as I wonder, again, is Cole pushing himself too hard?

Is this level of commitment sustainable?

Desperate for the distraction, I head to the Art Attic and lose myself in the studio. It's late when I arrive home, my messages to Cole unanswered.

Frowning, I call his cell. My concern spikes as I catch his voicemail.

Is something wrong? Or is he just tired? It makes sense that after the grueling workouts he's been doing, he'd pass out early. I press the worry down into the pit of my stomach and join my brothers as they play cards and drink beers in Gran's kitchen.

It's nearly 1 AM when Gran decides to whip up a banana bread. I try to stay present in the moment, in the laughing and joking with my brothers since it's a rarity for all of us to be home.

But I can't ignore the concern eating at the lining of my stomach.

When I wake up in the morning with no word from Cole, I know something is truly wrong.

TWENTY
COLE

MY HEART IS in my throat the entire flight to Wisconsin. My palms are sweaty, my skin too tight for my frame, my stomach swimming with nausea.

Uncle Kirk fell. I close my eyes as if that will block out Jamie's voice, her hysterical cry and nonsensical words, from my mind. The man has performed every type of manual labor since I was a kid and the fact that I didn't clue in that at nearly seventy, he shouldn't be climbing ladders and walking along the edges of roofs, makes me feel like garbage. Especially when all Uncle Kirk ever did was look out for me, raise me, love me.

I glare out the window of the plane, wishing it could move faster. Wishing I was there already, in the too clean hospital room with Jamie and Uncle Kirk, breathing in the same antiseptic smell from the night I lost my parents.

I left in such a hurry; I don't even know what I packed. I just need to get to Madison; I need to see my uncle. I need to be with my family and support them. Shit! Thinking of family reminds me that Bea's is all staying at Gran's. Her showcase is this weekend, and her brothers are all showing up for her.

I've never been prouder of my girl than when she invited

her brothers to her showcase. Now, the hard work she's poured into her craft for the past five weeks is coming to fruition and—am I going to be back in time to see it? To celebrate her?

My emotions are in overdrive. For an even-keeled guy, I feel out of control. I can't get a handle on my erratic thoughts, each one leading me down a new path filled with concerns.

Will Uncle Kirk need additional surgeries? How will this injury affect his mental health? Who will care for him?

Will I play well at my next game? Is my head too fucked up now to continue the streak I was blazing? Will the team see my commitment to my family as a distraction? Are they concerned? Coach Scotch was understanding but how long will that last? He has a team to run, and I have a commitment to maintain.

And Bea! Fuck, I didn't even call her. How could I? I was frantic, desperate to get on a flight, any flight that would move me closer to Uncle Kirk. Will she hate me if I miss her showcase? Will I hate myself for not supporting her the way I promised?

My throat constricts, a tightness that makes it difficult to breathe.

Uncle Kirk fell from a second-story balcony. He's currently in surgery, at least he was, at the time of wheels up. His doctors are confident that he'll survive, but his injuries were extensive—shattered pelvis, blown-out knees, lower back and hip injuries. I want to throw up just thinking about it.

My knee bounces up and down as I tap my fingertips against the windowpane. I'm jittery and scared, uncentered and helpless. I need a run, a lift, something to release this frantic energy coursing throughout my body. I clench my phone—turned to airplane mode—in my hand. Has Jamie been updated by the surgeon? Has Bea hit me up a thousand times? Did the team have a good practice?

Jesus, how many more hours is this damn flight?

"I'M OKAY, KID." Those are the first words Uncle Kirk speaks to me when he opens his eyes and sees me, panicked, sitting beside his hospital bed.

I breathe a sigh of relief, tears pricking the corners of my eyes. He's been out for a long stretch of time and while his injuries are extensive, they're not nearly as bad as originally believed. In fact, once the surgeons got him into the OR, his prognosis improved. "Uncle Kirk," I mutter. I move closer to his bedside and grasp his hand.

He grimaces as he shifts in bed. Immediately, I call for the nurse. "What do you need?"

"To piss."

I snort.

A nurse enters the room and smiles. "It's good to see you awake, Mr. Philips."

He smiles back at her, tossing me a wink. He's either high on pain meds or really hanging onto his humor, both of which are positive scenarios in this moment. The nurse asks me to leave for a moment, and I step into the hallway as she assists Uncle Kirk with his catheter and explains what the next few days will look like.

I debate calling Jamie but after a long night sitting in the OR waiting room, I know she's passed out. Since Uncle Kirk seems all right and Jamie needs her sleep, I hold off on the phone call. Instead, I kick my foot up behind me, rest against the wall, and scroll through the list of messages on the screen of my phone.

Most of them are from Bea. I sent her a quick text when I landed letting her know there's been a family emergency, but I haven't called her yet. What would I say? I had no updates on Uncle Kirk's condition and there's nothing she could have done for me anyway. I wouldn't even know what to ask of her.

"Cole," she answers immediately, the worry in her voice squeezing my chest.

"Hey," I say, not sounding like myself.

"Where are you? What happened?"

I close my eyes, pinching the skin above my eyebrow. "I'm home. In Wisconsin."

"Wisconsin?" She frowns. "I thought you were from Michigan."

I clear my throat. "Nah, just went to college there."

A tense beat of silence follows. "Is everything okay?"

I swear softly. "Uncle Kirk just woke up."

"Baby, what happened?"

I take a shaky breath, trying to keep the emotion out of my tone. "My uncle fell. Two stories. It's bad, Bea." I fill her in on everything I know about Uncle Kirk's prognosis which isn't much. Just that it's going to be a six-to-eight-month recovery time which will require a great deal of hands-on support.

Should I move him to Tennessee? Will he allow me to hire the support he needs to stay in his home? Can I afford it? Can I travel back and forth to see him? How frequently? Will it be enough?

"Cole." Bea's voice is calm, soothing.

I try to focus on her. God, I miss her. If I asked her to come, would she? No, I can't ask her that. Not when the biggest break of her career is happening in a handful of days. I clear my throat. "Yeah, Bea?"

"Talk to me. Please," her voice cracks and I feel worse.

But I don't know what to say. I don't know what to do. I'm so far out of my element, I feel like I'm drowning. The pressure is bearing down on me and I'm underwater, trying to swim against a damn riptide.

How the hell is Uncle Kirk going to afford his recovery with the additional support required? And the time off work?

God, I hope he accepts my support. How can I convince him it's not charity? It's just family helping family.

"I gotta go, Bea," I say. "I want to help my uncle and it's going to be hard to convince him to accept it."

"Okay," she says quietly, her disappointment evident. "Know that I'm here for you, Cole. Please, if you want to talk, call me."

"You've got your showcase to get ready for," I remind her. Now is not the time for Bea to be distracted. She needs to lock in and focus.

She needs to prove them all wrong.

"I love you, Cole," she tries again, breaking my heart in the process. What does she want from me? What does she expect me to say?

I open my mouth, but no words come out.

"I'm here for you," she repeats.

My eyes screw closed. "I know, Bea. I love you, too. Focus on your pottery, yeah?"

"Yeah," she murmurs, unconvinced. "I'll check in on you later."

"Okay, thanks." I disconnect the call and tap my head back against the wall.

My chest is too tight, my hands and feet tingling. I feel strange, like my body is going to cave in on itself. I open my mouth and gulp in oxygen, suddenly out of breath. Panic spreads throughout my body as I think about losing Uncle Kirk. About losing Bea. About losing everything I've worked so hard to achieve.

The fragility of life hits me like a steamroller, flattening me to the floor until I feel faint, black dots swimming in my peripheral vision. I sink to the floor and try to calm my racing heart, my spiraling thoughts.

Everything is fine; I'm okay. Bea will understand. My coaches will understand. Right now, my priority is Uncle Kirk. His care and making sure it's the best that exists, no matter the cost. I need to put my family first, the same way they always did for me.

My phone buzzes in my hand and I frown when I read my agent's name on the screen. What does he want?

Working a swallow, I answer. "Hey, Reg. This isn't a great time."

"I need two minutes of your time, Cole. You don't want to pass this up," he says.

I close my eyes again, wondering what the hell he's talking about. "Pass what up?"

"Cincinnati wants to buy your contract. And they're offering a lot of money for you. A fucking lot."

My eyes pop open. Cincinnati? They have a shitty reputation for spitting players out, used up and overworked. But right now, my family can use the money. Right now, I need to step up as the provider. Can I negotiate contract incentives? Would playing for a more established team result in endorsement deals? My mind whirs as I latch onto something I understand—the world of hockey.

Right now, this is something productive I can focus on. Control. "Tell me about the deal."

"YOU HOLDING UP OKAY?" Bodhi asks the morning of my showcase.

"If okay is wanting to vomit in my purse, then yes." I stare at my reflection in the mirror, skimming my hands over my hips. Dressed in a skirt, blouse, and sandals, I look professional but artsy. I tuck some errant curls behind my ears. My earrings are bright yellow. I made them and they make me smile. They're quirky, like me, and give the extra boost of confidence I need to shine today.

Bodhi comes into my room and closes the door. "You got this, Bea. This is what you worked for. I know it's scary but anything worthwhile is."

"I know." I turn to look at him. "I know you're right."

"Of course, I'm right." He winks. "Is Cole coming to the house or are we meeting him in Knoxville?"

"I'm not sure yet," I admit slowly, not wanting Bodhi to think badly of Cole. But Cole's been mentally MIA all week. While I know he's worried about his uncle, rightfully so, I also don't know much beyond that because he hasn't confided in me. Instead, he's checked out, turning inward instead of leaning on the love and support I'm trying to give him.

"Everything okay?" Bodhi asks gently, his expression devoid of judgement.

I sigh. "I'm sure Beau told you about Cole's uncle's accident."

"Yeah." Bodhi sits on the edge of my bed.

I wring my hands, pacing back and forth as I admit, "I don't know much else. Cole's been distant since it happened. I mean, he didn't even tell me he was flying to Wisconsin"—I bug my eyes out at my brother—"and he just got back this morning. He's gotta be exhausted. I can't get a read on him; he's barely confiding in me."

"Everyone processes things differently, Bea."

"I know that."

"Cole might be more of a silent processor," my brother continues, pointing out the possibility gently since I process by talking everything out. Usually with Celine. "He could be trying to wrap his head around things with his uncle and *not* wanting to burden you with it since he knows how important today is to you."

"Yeah," I agree, trying to give Cole the benefit of the doubt.

But him not letting me in over the past few days hurts. For the first time, it feels like we aren't in this, our relationship, together. It feels like we're moving at two different speeds, in two different directions. I want him to let me support him the way he consistently shows up for me. Instead, I'm met with his silence or a brush-off.

My thoughts have been tied up on Cole. My nerves twisted about what he's feeling, about what he's thinking, about where I factor into any of it in his mind. And I'd be lying if I said a teeny tiny slice of me wasn't resentful. This is a huge week for me and without the reassurance of Cole's presence, it's been hard to focus and lose myself the way I usually can in my craft. It's selfish as hell but I know if he'd let me in, I could help him. Giving him support, knowing where his head's at, would also ease my concerns and let me focus on the showcase the way he keeps telling me to.

My phone beeps and I sigh when I read the text. "He's meeting us in Knoxville."

Bodhi stands. "Today's about you, Bea. You earned this. Focus on your next move and block out all the noise."

"Okay," I say softly.

"You look beautiful, Bea. Like an artist."

I chuckle. "It's the earrings, isn't it?"

He laughs and holds out his arms. I step into his embrace and breathe in my brother's strength as he hugs me tightly. "Let's do this," I say.

"Thatta girl."

THE EVENT SPACE IS PACKED. Artists and creatives have taken over downtown Knoxville, putting on one hell of a showcase that highlights every medium of art. I can't contain my excitement as I drink in the paintings, the pottery, the drawings and demonstrations. It's colorful and textured, bursting with energy and light.

"Wow!" Brody spins in a circle. "This is something else, Bea."

"Thanks for coming," I tell my family.

Gran pinches my ass. "As if we'd miss it."

I grin at the pride in her voice and press a kiss to her temple. "Love you, Gran."

"You were born to shine, bumblebee," she whispers, using the nickname I haven't heard since my parents passed. It's what Dad called me and hearing it today, in this moment, brings tears to my eyes and pride to my heart.

"Thanks, Gran."

Blake links his arm with Gran's and points to a vendor he wants to check out. As he leads Gran away, he shoots me a wink.

"Thank you," I mouth to him. I pull out my phone, my heart sinking that there's no message, no good luck, no anything, from Cole.

> **CELINE**
>
> Rooting for you, Bea!
>
> **NOELLE**
>
> Good luck today!
>
> **IZZY**
>
> Proud of you! I'll be stopping by to purchase all your vases!

Where the hell is my boyfriend?

"Bea?" Brody says.

I look up. Seeing the concern shadowing his eyes forces me into action. I slip my phone into my purse and gesture toward my booth. "You guys check it out. I need to get to my booth and talk to Mel."

"Do you, Bea. We'll see you in a bit," Beau says.

I wave to my family, push Cole from my mind, and track down Mel.

"This turnout is unreal!" I tell her.

"Bea!" She clasps my shoulders, pulling me in for a quick hug. "I can't tell you how many people have been inquiring about your pottery. Come, I must introduce you." She whisks me into a group of art enthusiasts and the next few hours pass in a blur of introductions, explanations of my pottery, and storytelling.

I'm so caught up in the moment that it takes me a minute to see Cole standing with Bodhi and Beau on the periphery of my booth.

"Thank you so much for taking the time to come today." I shake hands with an elderly gentleman.

"You're very talented, Bea. It's a pleasure to make your acquaintance," he replies.

"Likewise." I grin, waving goodbye before I make my way to Cole.

"You're here!" I exclaim, going up on my tippytoes to kiss him.

He nods, avoiding my lips and pressing a quick kiss to my cheek instead. What the hell? I pull back, frowning at him, but he doesn't meet my eyes. Does he not want to kiss me in front of my brothers?

"Cole." I shake his arm, trying to understand his stand-offish behavior.

"Hey," he mutters. He finally meets my gaze and I suck in a breath.

He looks pale. His eyes are bloodshot, rimmed in red. Exhaustion clings to his expression, grief pressed into the lines of his face.

He lifts his chin toward my bustling booth. "Congratulations, Bea. You're very popular."

I frown at his word choice; I step back from the hard edge in his tone. What the hell does that mean?

Cole shakes off my touch and points to another booth. "Do your thing. I'll be around."

As he lopes off, completely uninterested in my work, I try to make sense of his actions. Did something happen? Is he okay? It's so unlike Cole to not celebrate my success with me that panic for his well-being rushes through me. "Cole!" I call out, needing to look in his eyes and—what?—gain some reassurance that he's okay? That we're okay?

I step in his direction, but he's swallowed up by a crowd. As I near, I see that he's signing autographs, offering smiles that don't reach his eyes, and lighthearted quips to a group of fans. I frown, waffling between interjecting and returning to my booth. Do we talk now or later?

"He's got a long going on," Beau whispers as he comes up beside me. But he stares hard at Cole, just as confused by his behavior as I am.

"Yeah," I say, hurt and worried by Cole's attitude.

"Bea!" a familiar voice rings out.

"You came!" I turn toward my college roommate Izzy as she collides with me. We clutch each other, laughing hysterically.

"You're killing it, girl. Of course, I came to cheer you on. I'm so damn proud of you." Iz squeezes my shoulders. She turns me back toward my booth and I let her pull me along. Cole and I will talk later.

Should I try to introduce my old roommate to my boyfriend? I glance behind me but Cole is gone.

I shake the thought from my head and swallow back the frustration coating my tongue.

Izzy leans in close. "A few of the board members for the Landry Artistic Achievement program are here."

My eyes widen. "Seriously?"

Izzy nods, her fingertips digging into my skin. She's buzzing with energy. "Yes!" she squeaks. "Mom's talking to a few, and Bea, they're all mentioning your name."

"Shut up," I mutter, feeling my body freeze. The Landry Artistic Achievement program! Imagine? No, no way. Saying my name and offering me a position are two vastly different things. I can't get my hopes up. I won't get my hopes up. I—

"Imagine if they invite you?" Izzy squeals.

I clutch Izzy's arm. "I can't." I shake my head. The program is four months long, just outside of Nashville. Right now, I can't think of leaving because I can't think of anything except talking to Cole. Did he go home? Is he walking around? Is he okay?

Don't give up on your daydreams for anyone. Noelle DiSanto's voice rings in my head. I take a deep breath. Right now, I need to get through the showcase and give this afternoon my all.

I lose Izzy as I'm pulled into other conversations. With her mention of the program buzzing in my mind, I block out Cole and his distracting behavior. Instead, I focus on this moment. I engage with every person who looks at my pieces, who poses a question, who has an idea they want to discuss.

The hours roll into each other as my booth maintains a steady stream of visitors. As the afternoon seeps into evening and the crowd dies down, my feet ache from standing all day. My voice is hoarse from so much chatting. I've never felt better. Alive.

Renewed energy in my future and excitement for my pottery fills me to the brim. I'm dancing on clouds of exhilaration when a man clears his throat. I turn toward the sound and grin at the elderly gentleman from earlier, holding his hat in his hand.

"You're back!" I smile.

He chuckles and nods. "Sure am."

"Did you enjoy the showcase?"

"A great deal." He shuffles closer, his smile widening. "I'm Jeffery Landry."

My throat dries and my palms feel clammy. Both hot and cold beads burst over my skin, making me shiver. Jeffery Landry, head of the Landry Artistic Achievement Foundation, head of the program, is standing in my booth. He's talking to me!

I resist the urge to pinch myself and make sure this is real. Is this really happening?

Mr. Landry's eyes soften. "You're exceptionally talented, Bea. Your pottery is genuine and raw, evoking more emotion than I've seen in a long time. But it's your personality that shines. I'm glad we were able to chat earlier. Now that I've met you, I see what the hype is about."

Hype? What hype? Oh my God. Oh my God. Oh my God.

A bumblebee swarms around me for a moment before disappearing and I smile. This moment is meant to be. This moment is going to change my life.

"I'd like to invite you into our program," Mr. Landry offers.

Tears fills my eyes as gratitude swells in my chest. "I'm honored," I whisper, too overcome with emotion to expand.

Mr. Landry smiles. "You know it's a vigorous program, focused on craftsmanship and mentoring."

"I know," I say.

"It's four months long, away from home."

"Yes."

"We start in two weeks. You're the last invitee."

"Thank you."

He chuckles and grips his hat. "Do you accept, Bea?"

"I do," I say without a second thought. My daydream is becoming a reality and I need to put that first. Isn't that what Cole would say? Isn't that what my brothers have done in their professional lives?

Last week, I would have needed Cole's support. Last week, I'd have wanted my brothers' opinions. Last week, I'd worry about Gran and the house and a million other things.

But today, I'm seizing the opportunity with the knowledge that everything will be sorted. Today, I'm saying yes. I hold out a hand to Mr. Landry. "Thank you, sir. This opportunity means the world to me."

He shakes my hand again and nods. "I can't wait to see the artist you evolve into."

I smile. "Me too." *But I'm kind of loving the woman.*

TWENTY-TWO

COLE

CINCINNATI WILL DOUBLE MY SALARY. Fucking double it, overnight. Just like that, all of Uncle Kirk's medical issues, the cost of care, the additional help, the time off work, goes away. Just like that I have salary incentives and a better shot with endorsements. I can step up and provide for my family, the way they've always given to me.

But fuck. I nearly plow into a hippy-looking woman with purple feathers in her ears.

"You okay, dude?" She frowns, looking at me like I'm an alien. At least she's not asking for an autograph. The group that swarmed me earlier came out of nowhere and while it's one of the most flattering things to happen to me, I'm not in the right headspace to enjoy it.

"Sorry," I mutter, brushing past her. Where the hell am I? I spin in a circle. Booths and stands, colors and patterns, paintings and chimes, spin in my line of vision. Where's Bea's booth? Where's my girl?

I move to the edge of the street and scan the event. It's much bigger than I anticipated, with art connoisseurs, aspiring artists, and curious families mixing. I already know everyone who enters Bea's booth will be impressed. She's talented and this showcase is going to land her on the map. What opportunities will arise from today?

Will she stay here, in Knoxville? She promised she'd care for Gran so I don't know how she can go anywhere else. But she's always been honest about desiring more, about having experiences away from home.

If I move to Ohio, will our relationship work? How can it, with that much distance between us? Shit, if I turn down this offer, am I doing it for Bea? The thought unsettles me because she's the reason I would stay.

Well, her and the Thunderbolts. The Cincinnati Serpents are tough. There's no value for loyalty. There's no family culture. They don't have teambuilding sessions and field days. They pay money, demand perfection, and cut you when you fuck up.

I close my eyes again. Do I want to live under that type of pressure? Can I handle it?

If Uncle Kirk wasn't laid out in the hospital right now, would the money be worth it?

"Hey!" Someone jostles my shoulder.

I open my eyes and see Beau.

"What's going on with you today?" He frowns, his eyes narrowed with an edge of frustration. Of course, he's annoyed; I'm not showing up for Bea the way I promised. The way I'm capable of.

I heave out a sigh, debating if I should tell him about my offer. I have to decide by tomorrow if I'm going to take it. Double the pay, but lose my girl. Help Uncle Kirk, but let down my team.

Would Beau understand? As former military, part of me thinks he would understand better than any of the other guys. He must have made tough calls; he must live with regrets. But my situation is different than any other guy on the team because I'm dating his sister. He has to care for her happiness over my financial stability.

Beau sighs. "Bea was offered a spot in the Landry Artistic Achievement program."

"What's that?"

He shakes his head. "Fuck if I know. It's prestigious as hell. Four months living on some commune outside of Nashville, creating and being mentored all day."

She's leaving? Of course she is. The opportunities are already coming in; she's earned them. "Is she gonna take it?"

Beau sizes me up. "Does it matter?"

"Of course it fucking matters," I growl, yanking the back of my neck. If I stay and she leaves...but I can't put that pressure on her. I'm either staying because I want to or leaving because it's the right thing to do. For my family.

"You either love her or you don't, Rookie. A couple of hours shouldn't make or break y'all."

"Yeah," I mutter. Because Knoxville to Nashville isn't a big deal. But what about Cincinnati to Nashville? Would that break us?

"She *should* take it," Beau mutters. "She's worked hard as hell for this chance. She's been grinding a long time for this opportunity. I had no idea how passionate she is about it." He shakes his head. "Or how talented. It'd be a waste if she turns it down, but all Bodhi told me was that she was invited. I don't know what she's decided."

"Why wouldn't she take it?" I mutter, my stomach sinking.

Now Beau's looking at me like I'm an alien. "First, Gran."

I nod. "Right."

"But you want to know the real reason I can see her passing it up?"

I freeze, knowing what he's going to say and not wanting to hear it.

"You." Beau's words land like a punch to the gut. "The shit you're pulling today is messing with her head. Now maybe you've got your own stuff going on—" He holds up a hand when I open my mouth. "But the fact that you're here and not giving Bea the support she earned is fucked up. I hope she accepts the invite and does the program." He stalks off, his anger visible in the bunching of his shoulders.

"I do too," I tell his retreating back. Beau doesn't hear me.

But I do. It's as if now that I've said the words aloud, I know what I need to do. I need to man up. I need to provide for my family, support my girlfriend, and do what needs to be done.

I'm not selfish. Or washed up. Or spiteful. I'm not my father.

With that thought looping in my mind, I send Bea a text.

COLE

Hey. Something came up and I need to leave. Talk later? Proud of you today...

BEA

You okay?

COLE

Yeah. We need to talk.

I wince as soon as I send it.

BEA

Okay. I'll come by later.

COLE

OK.

I don't want to ruin any more of Bea's day, so I take off. I let her revel in her moment. I hope she's dreaming about the possibilities of this new art program. Instead, I shut my emotional shit down and start to pack.

THE KNOCK on my door is tentative and the hesitancy behind it twists my stomach. She knows I'm going to deliver bad news and I fucking hate myself for all the things I'm going to say. But she needs to take this opportunity. And I need to take this offer.

I pull the door open, my heart swelling into my throat at the uncertainty, the naked vulnerability, on Bea's face.

"Come on in." I hold the door wider. "Are you hungry?"

She shakes her head and enters my kitchen. "Gran took us all out for milkshakes and burgers." A small smile flits across her face and I wonder if she's remembering something from when she was a kid. I'm glad she has those happy childhood memories to sustain her when things go sideways. I wish I had more of them.

Bea crosses her arms over her chest. "What's going on?"

"Congratulations on today."

"Thank you." Her tone is clipped, and I hear the hurt underneath it.

"I'm proud of you," I try again.

She arches an eyebrow. "You have a funny way of showing it."

I sigh and pull out a chair at the dining table.

Bea does the same and sits down across from me. "I'm worried about you, Cole."

I disregard her concern. It makes me feel worse for the news I'm about to share. "I want you to take the invitation for that art program."

Surprise cuts across her face. "Beau told you."

"Yes."

"Okay. Well, I already accepted."

"Good," I breathe out.

Bea frowns at me. "Cole, it's only for four months and I'll be right outside of Nashville. It's not that big of a deal. I mean, the program is huge. But the long-distance part isn't really long-distance at all." She shakes her head. "Besides, I want to talk about you. About your extra workouts, the way you've been pushing yourself, your uncle's injury. I want you to trust me with the big things and that's not going to change because of this program."

God, she's breaking my heart. I look down, steel my expression, and clear my throat before meeting her gaze again.

Realization colors her expression and she gasps. "Do you think we won't make it? Do you…do you not want to *try*?"

"I'm moving to Ohio."

"What?" she shouts.

"My agent called a few days ago. It's an offer I can't pass up." I keep my voice even, my tone measured.

Bea scoffs, her cheeks blazing red. "Really? Because they're a better team?"

I shrug. "It's a smart move for my career."

"Your career." She shakes her head, disappointed. In a flash, her worry morphs into anger. "What about the team you're part of here? What about the guys who have invested in you from the beginning? You're just going to turn your back on them because another team has more wins? Or is offering you more money?"

At the mention of money, I get defensive. "It's money my uncle needs, Bea."

"Oh!" She throws a hand in the air. "So now you're being self-sacrificing, is that it?"

"Don't judge what you don't understand," I say through clenched teeth. "You always knew this was a possibility."

"Of course, I did. I even expected it," she hollers.

"What?"

"A trade? Sure. But you breaking up with me because long-distance sounds hard? No, Cole. I didn't see that coming." She stands. "Is that it? You really want to end this?"

I stand too. My heart rate is erratic. My hands feel tingly and there's a buzzing in my eardrums. *No! I don't want to end this!* The words explode in my head, but I can't say them. Because I need to do what's best for Uncle Kirk. I need to do what's best for Bea. "I think it's for the best."

"Right." She nods, moving toward the door. "I'm glad you're so caught up on proving everyone wrong, Cole." She pauses at the door and looks at me over her shoulder. "You proved me wrong too. I really thought I could trust you. I really believed we had a future. I let myself *love* you, Cole." Then, she leaves my house and slams the door behind her.

It echoes for a second and then, silence settles. I drop back into my chair feeling like I'm going to throw up. I just let Bea go. I let her walk away. Hell, I practically asked her to. If this is for the best, why does it feel like the worst decision I've ever made?

Why does it feel like a fucking mistake?

"ARE you out of your fucking mind?" Uncle Kirk hollers the second I answer his call.

"What happened? What's wrong?" Panic unravels through my limbs.

"That's what I want to ask you."

"Huh?"

"Huh? That's all you got?"

"Uncle Kirk, what are you talking about?" I relax a little that he's clearly annoyed with me, a good sign considering the alternative.

"Jamie told me you're considering the Serpents," he hisses.

"Oh," I sigh. Of course, Jamie told him. Even though I asked her not to, a part of me knew she would. Is that why I told her? Because subconsciously, I don't *want* to leave the Bolts. And Uncle Kirk knows that. So does Jamie.

"Yeah, oh," Uncle Kirk mimics my voice.

I crack a grin. "It's a good offer."

"With a shit team."

"They're having a good season."

"I'm not talking about their ranking, and you know it. Come on kid, do you really want to give up everything you've achieved for a paycheck?"

"Lots of people work jobs they don't love for a paycheck. At least I love my job," I retort.

"But you don't have to. Right now, you love your job, and you love your team. Your coaches, your city, your girl."

I wince at the reminder of Bea. "We broke up." I don't know why I tell him. He's confined to a bed, battling excruciating pain, worrying about my future, and I tell him about my breakup with Bea. Maybe because I know he'll weigh in on that too.

"Because of the Serpents?" His tone is less hostile than a moment ago.

"She got accepted into a prestigious art program."

"Good for her. Is it on the moon?"

"No," I snort.

"A decade commitment?"

I roll my eyes. "Four months."

"And she didn't want to try to make it work?"

I blow out a sigh. He knows it was me. He knows me. "My call." I clear my throat.

"So, it's because of the Serpents."

"I guess so."

"Ah, kid. Your heart's too big and you try too damn hard to protect it. I get it. Given your childhood, the whole damn mess of it, of course you protect yourself. But you try to protect everyone else too. I don't want you to take the offer with the Serpents. Unless you're doing it for yourself, one-hundred percent, because you think it's necessary for your career, I don't want you to take it."

"It doubles my pay."

"So what?"

I exhale, trying to word this delicately, in a way that won't offend my uncle. "Uncle Kirk, your recovery—"

"Is taken care of."

"Your loss of wages—"

"Are taken care of."

"What?" I ask, not understanding. The medical bills Uncle Kirk incurred are staggering. Coupled with his inability to work, I don't see how anything is taken care of.

"My employer is covering everything. The fall happened on the job, due to negligence."

"What's that mean?" I ask.

"The guy I was working with was drunk. The accident was avoidable," he sighs.

"Shit." Anger races through me on my uncle's behalf. "That never should have happened."

"Except it did," he sighs, resigned. "And it could have been a lot worse. I'm grateful to be here, kid. And you know what?"

"What?"

"Maybe this time laid out is good for me. It will give me the chance to slow down and reflect."

I take the phone away from my ear and stare at it. What the hell is Uncle Kirk talking about?

"You get to be my age," he continues, "you see things differently. I look at you, Cole, and I'm so damn proud of the man you are. Don't waste your happiness on a paycheck. Don't throw away a woman you could truly love, build a life with, on a career move. You'll regret both every damn time."

His words are sobering. Partly because it's unlike him to be introspective. Partly because they ring with truth; it makes me uneasy.

I messed everything up with Bea. I was so intent on doing what I *thought* was best, I never stopped to consider what *is* best. What about her thoughts? Her feelings or ideas for the future? Fuck, I thought my love for her was the sacrifice. Instead, I sacrificed *us*. I hurt her.

What the hell was I thinking?

Bea's anger, her pain, blares through my mind. "What if it's too late?"

"It's not."

"I hurt her. Pushed her away."

"So? Reel her back in."

"She's not a fish, Uncle Kirk. You think it's that easy?" I bite out.

Uncle Kirk chuckles. "Hell no. It's gonna be hell, Cole. Hell. But if you really love her, you'll stick it out. And prove her right."

I close my eyes at his word choice. What did Bea say? I proved her wrong by allowing her to think she could trust me?

My throat burns and my eyes sting from my own stupidity. How could I allow my Bea to think I'm untrustworthy? To question my love for her.

Prove her right. "Got any ideas?"

My uncle chuckles again. "You'll figure it out, Cole. You always do."

TWENTY-THREE
BEA

I HIDE my phone under my pillow so I don't have to read Celine's threat. The fact that she would willingly seek out Beau shows how concerned she is. Beau's concerned too. And Gran. My brothers.

I'm too numb to be concerned. I'm just tired. And hurt. And achingly sad.

How could Cole give up on us, on me, so easily? How could he throw it all away because of a little long-distance? Four months isn't long. And if he takes the trade, so what? We live in a modern era with daily flights. We would have made it work.

I loved—stupid tears—*love* him.

For the first time, I feel truly sorry for Jay. Is this how he felt? Did I gut him the same way Cole gutted me? Holy shit, is this karma? Did I bring this awful breakup on myself by letting Jay go?

No, Jay and I were over for years. But then why did Cole end us? Why was it so easy for him to cut me off? Were my feelings stronger than his? Did the novelty of dating the quirky potter wear off?

What happened?

A knock sounds on my bedroom door and I groan into my pillow. Maybe if I pretend I'm sleeping, Gran will leave me alone.

I close my eyes and try to even out my breathing. The door creaks open.

"Cut the shit; I know you're awake," Beau says.

I open my eyes and sigh. "How'd you know?"

"Your nose wiggles when you're fake sleeping."

I rub the tip of my nose. "How long have you known that?"

"Since you were eleven."

"Damn," I mutter, recalling all the times Beau's called me out.

Beau sits on the edge of my bed. "You okay?"

"I'm still here." I throw a hand out to the side.

Beau gives me a sympathetic smile. "That's not what I asked."

My tears come, as if on cue, and splatter onto my cheeks.

Beau pulls me into his arms, and I sniffle and sob on his shoulder, my body shaking with the waves of pain at losing Cole. At Cole letting me go. At him giving up on us.

Beau rubs my back and makes soothing sounds, the same way he did when I was younger. The year we lost our parents, I woke nightly, screaming from night terrors, sobbing from grief. Every night, Beau would hold me, let me cry it out, and promise it would be a teeny bit easier in the morning, if only because the sun came up.

"You're going to be okay, Bea."

"I know," I say, wiping my eyes. I pull away and give him a pathetic smile. "But it hurts real bad."

Anguish cuts through his eyes. "I know," he says. He does know, losing Celine broke him in a way he never recovered from. "It will be a tiny bit better in the morning."

"If only because the sun comes up?"

He snorts. "Exactly." He wipes my tears from my cheeks. "But also because Cole fucked up, and he knows it."

I shake my head.

"He's a mess, Bea," Beau says gently.

"Good."

My brother rolls his lips together to keep from grinning. "You don't mean that."

I avert my gaze because he's right, I don't mean it. But I want to mean it, dammit! I want to want Cole to feel as miserable as I do right now.

"He was worried about his uncle," Beau tries again. "Look…" He touches my knee to get my attention. I turn my gaze back to him. "I don't know much of Cole's story. But I know he had to grow up quickly. I know he's had to live in survival mode for a long time. And I know that the feelings he has for you, he's never had them before. Does that ring true?"

I clear my throat but tip my head in agreement.

"Put all that together and sometimes, when things are

complicated, when things feel uncertain, a guy like that will try to fix them. He'll try to make things certain. He'll look to control the situation on his terms and live up to all the things he's striving to be. Cole fucked up big-time, Bea. But I don't think he meant to hurt you."

I stare at Beau for a long time. How much is he speaking about Cole, and how much is he talking about himself? Finally, I agree, "I don't think he meant to hurt me either."

Beau lets out a breath, relieved that I'm seeing reason.

"But he did." I fall back to my pillow and close my eyes. "You can close the door on your way out."

"You gotta eat, Bea."

"Not hungry. What I need to do is pack." I smooth my palms over my bedspread, feeling that restless tingle that means I need to create. "Pour myself into pottery."

Beau gives me a long, searching look. "Just don't lose yourself, Bea. Don't shut down because you're hurting."

I nod even though I'm already numb. I've already shut down.

But I appreciate Beau's words of advice so I tell him, "Thanks for being my big brother, Beau."

"I love you, bumblebee."

I smile sadly at the old nickname. "Love you too."

"There's a plate in the microwave for you." He gets up and walks toward my bedroom door. "Gran made you mac and cheese."

Comfort food. "Thanks."

The door closes behind Beau, and I let out a sigh. My heart feels broken, my confidence shattered. But I still have my family. I still have my art.

And when I climb out of bed at midnight and dig into the mac and cheese, I realize that's enough.

That tomorrow, the sun will come up and it will hurt a teeny bit less.

TWENTY-FOUR
COLE

I SHOOT pucks at the net for no reason other than I need to get out of my head. I'm not much of a shooter, but the rhythmic slap of the blade against the puck, the sting that travels up my arm from the impact, the puck cutting through the air, is comforting.

For all the things I've fucked up in my life, I've never messed up hockey. This week, I almost did. I almost signed with a team that wouldn't have cared about me as a person. To the Serpents, I would have been a player, one who brings value until I don't. My streak would have had to have been endless. The pressure, nonstop. The management wouldn't have invested in my growth, personally or professionally. They wouldn't have an open-door policy, one I could utilize any time.

Uncle Kirk was right. The paycheck never would have been worth it. There is no amount of money, no status, no network big enough to justify tainting the only thing that's brought me peace. Hockey has been my salvation.

At least, until Bea. But I fucked that up.

When I called my agent to turn down the offer, I did so knowing I'm staying in Tennessee for the right reasons. The

Thunderbolts, hockey, my career. But I'd be lying if I didn't wish I could earn Bea back. Her trust, her love, her admiration.

Knowing I let her down cuts deep because she's the last person I want to disappoint. She's the only woman I ever cared about hurting. I did both.

The puck bounces off the crossbar and I swear.

"I saw you this morning," Beau calls out as he glides onto the ice.

I glare at him. Can't a guy get some peace to wallow by himself? I've got the whole team up in my business, giving me shit for breaking Bea's heart, and now, another talk with Beau?

"She won't see me," I respond, even though I'm sure he knows that. I've sat on Gran's front porch for the past five mornings without catching a glimpse of Bea. I knock on the door, and it remains unanswered, even though I spot Gran peeking out. And three days ago, Beau. He must be sleeping at the house.

Two days ago, Gran left me a coffee. Yesterday, sweet tea and a muffin. Today, sweet tea, a muffin, and a fruit cup. "But Gran's sending mixed signals."

Beau smirks. "She doesn't want you to give up on Bea yet. Us Turners, we can hold a grudge."

I snort. "Bea isn't even reading my messages. I checked."

"She's hurt."

"I know."

"She trusted you."

"Right," I say through gritted teeth. "And I lost her trust."

"You're not going to earn it back by sitting on the porch."

"I just want to talk to her."

"You gotta speak her language."

"What the fuck does that mean?" I bite out. "My uncle, my cousin, you, Gran, the guys on the team—everyone's got an opinion and insight to offer but no one shares actual advice."

"You know." Beau skates past me, not bothering to look if I'm following. I am. We exit the ice and make our way back to the locker room. "When I first found out you were dating Bea, I was pissed. Not because I don't like you, but I didn't like you guys together. You're a hockey player with a short-term contract and a bright future. Hell, you'll probably make captain of a team before you're thirty. But Bea? In my mind, Bea was my kid sister, a little bit lost, a lot floundering. I worried she would get caught up in you and your career and lose sight of her own desires."

"I'd never let that happen."

"No." Beau shakes his head. "*She'd* never let that happen. Dating you gave her the confidence, the edge, to push for what she wants in life. I appreciate that about you, Rookie. I respect you. And I'm proud as hell of my sister. She's going to be one hell of an artist."

"She already is."

He tips his head in agreement. "She'll also be one hell of a wife."

I stop short. What is he saying?

"She's miserable without you, man. You're her one. Learn how to speak her language." Beau taps my arm before side-stepping me.

I stand in the hallway for a long time, trying to figure out what that means.

But when it clicks, it's suddenly the clearest thing in the entire world.

What's Bea's language? Pottery.

Pulling out my phone, I email the team.

Subject Line: Ready to Grovel

Then, I call Mel at the Art Attic and prepare to win back my girlfriend.

"I WISH THIS WAS MY CAREER," Damien Barnes mutters as his bowl comes into shape on the spinning wheel. "It's so fucking relaxing."

"Yeah, and potters make bank so there's no financial stress to worry about," Patton remarks, sarcastic as always. "I can't believe you considered shit from the Serpents." He shakes his head at me. "Don't you know they don't give two fucks?"

I sigh, hating that River Patton is right. "I got caught up on the paycheck, the contract incentives."

"Dude." Barnes shakes his head. "That's so unlike you."

"Because of your uncle?" Brawler asks, his age providing a lens of wisdom to this conversation.

"Yeah. He took me in as a kid, raised me as his own," I say, molding the clay the way Bea taught me. "I hate that he's laid up in a hospital bed. I want him to have whatever he needs."

"Took you in? Where were your parents?" Patton asks.

"Dead. They overdosed, meth, when I was ten." I think I have the shape right for a handle.

I glance up as silence descends over the small studio. Shit. Sometimes, I forget that my childhood sounds as tragic as it was. For me, it's been years since my parents passed and Uncle Kirk and Jamie gave me such a great life afterwards that I don't dwell much on those first ten years.

"Fuck," Patton mutters. "That's heavy, Rookie."

"I'd consider the Serpents too," Damien says, half apologizing for his earlier judgement.

I shrug. "My uncle would have kicked my ass if I did. He's doing much better than expected."

"You think you're not contributing to his care, but his not having to worry about you and your decisions helps take stress off his shoulders," Devon Hardt offers. "You made the right call."

"Thanks," I say, meaning it. "I made the choice to stay for me. For you guys, for the Bolts. But I desperately want Bea back. Even if I left, I would have tried to win her back and done the distance thing. She's it for me. I love her so fucking much and I hate myself for hurting her."

"Jesus," Patton mutters. "Just because we dipped our toe in your personal shit doesn't mean we want the whole fucking lake."

Brawler gives me a searching look, his eyes knowing. "Just keep showing up."

"I don't know," my voice shakes. Gran didn't leave me a coffee today. Is that a sign? "Her ex-boyfriend kept showing up and it wasn't what she wanted at all. How do I know when enough is enough?"

"You're not Jay," Beau tosses out.

Not much of a glowing endorsement but given the situation, I'll take it.

"This is your last-ditch effort," Damien says.

"Your big gesture," Devon adds.

"Go big or go home," River chuckles.

Shit, what if I do this and it isn't enough? What if I can't prove to Bea how much I love her? What if I do go home, heartbroken and empty?

"Jesus," River mutters again, shaking his head at me. "It's gonna work, Rookie. Have some fucking faith."

I never thought I'd take words of advice from River, but right now, that's exactly what I do. I let his outlook shore up my resolve. Then, I fire up the spinning wheel and get to work.

TWENTY-FIVE
BEA

MY SUITCASE HITS each step with a thud. A bang that rings with a finality and also, a promise; I'm chasing my passion.

"Hey, I got your bag." Blake appears at the foot of the stairs and reaches for my suitcase. I let him take it.

"Thanks." I plop my shoulder bag on top. "Are you sure you can stay here for four months? With everything you and Brody have going on, isn't it tough working from opposite sides of the country?"

"You worry too much, baby Bea. One of the perks of working in the tech sector means working from anywhere. And, when I have to fly back for meetings, Beau is here, or Bodhi can come up and keep Gran company." He tugs on the ends of my hair.

"Thanks, Blake." I hug my brother.

He keeps one arm around me as Gran shuffles into the foyer. "Besides"—he grins at Gran—"I signed me and Granny up for dance lessons."

"Oh, psh." She flicks her wrist at him. When he doesn't respond, she pauses. An expression I've rarely seen—wistful and longing and hopeful—ripples over her face.

I glance up at Blake, but his eyes are pinned to Gran.

"We start next Thursday," Blake says.

Emotion swells in Gran's eyes and her face transforms. A youthfulness blossoms in her cheeks and her eyes dance. "I know where my dancing shoes are."

Blake chuckles. "And I've dusted mine off. I'm ready for you, Gran."

"Try to keep up with me, Blake," she retorts.

It warms my heart to know that Gran and Blake will bond while I'm at the program. It's only four months. This is good for me; it's good for my family. I just wish it was good for me and Cole.

Thinking about him hurts. I know he's been reaching out, texting, calling, showing up, but I have nothing to say to him. The best thing I can do right now is push Cole Philips from my mind and pour the jagged edges of my broken heart into art. Take my pain and use it to create.

"Bring Cole a coffee," Gran says softly.

Blake snickers and I huff out a breath. "He's here?"

"Been here since six," Blake replies.

I glance at my watch. "It's ten."

"I know." Blake tugs my hair again, his expression unreadable. "You should talk to him before you leave. Any guy who sits on Gran's porch this many days in a row deserves a conversation."

"Put the neighbors out of their misery," Gran adds. "They can only take so many front yard shenanigans."

"We live in the country," I remind her, taking my suitcase from Blake. I drag it out to the porch and glare at my brother and Gran. "The car arrives in thirty minutes."

"Then you should start listening," Blake advises.

What the hell is wrong with him? Since he arrived in Tennessee a few days ago, he's seen me mope around the house in states of anger or devastating sadness. Now, he wants me to listen to Cole? "It's not going to change anything," I spit back, pushing the door open with my ass.

Blake winks but doesn't respond, which annoys me.

I step out onto the porch backwards, dragging my suitcase with me. No help from Blake this time. But Cole swoops in, his fingertips skimming the small of my back. "I got that," he says, taking the handle from me.

The moment our fingers brush, I release my hold and let him have it.

He settles my suitcase near the porch steps. I cross my arms over my chest, my hands splayed wide as if to protect myself.

But when I look up at Cole, I gasp. He looks awful. Exhaustion clings to his skin with dark smudges underneath his eyes. Eyes that are usually colored with mirth are burning with agony. He moves slowly, as if the constant energy he used to exude has left him. Stripped him bare until only a shell remains.

"Fuck, I love you, Bea," he mutters the words, gravelly in a tone I've never heard before. "I won't lose you. Not for being careless. Not for pushing you away. Not because I'm an idiot. If I lose you, I'll never forgive myself. And, Bea, I need to forgive myself. So please, just give me five minutes and hear me out? Let me try to make things right."

I was prepared to tell him to leave, but my words falter. Now that I'm standing here, staring at him, with my hands desperate to reach out and my heart stuttering in my chest, there's no way I can turn him away. I don't *want* to and that scares me almost as much as this burned-out version of Cole.

"Talk." Just because I feel for him doesn't mean I'm going to make it easy. Not when he shut me out when I worried about him. Not when he blindsided me on one of the most important days of my life.

Cole sighs and gestures toward the stairs. We both sit

down on the top step and I know this is a make it or break it moment, but I hold back my judgment until I hear Cole out.

"I've never been in love before," he starts, surprising me. I thought he was going to launch into an apology. "The way I feel for you, it consumes me. I think of you all the time. I want you, crave you, constantly. Until you, I filled every void in my life with hockey. Suddenly, I couldn't balance the two. How can I be my best on the ice and be my best with you, the way you deserve? I've been burning both ends of the candle for months, thinking I could handle it. With each new challenge, I pushed harder. But when Uncle Kirk fell..." He chews the corner of his mouth, his voice faltering. "Fuck, Bea. It messed with my head. My uncle is like my father. He's the only man in my life who consistently showed up for me. To see him in that hospital bed, laid out, unsure if he'd walk again, it gutted me. And then the medical bills? The financial strain? All I could think about was doing right by him, the way he's always done right by me.

"When my agent called with the offer from the Serpents, it seemed too good to be true. It was the answer to a prayer I'd silently been tossing up in Uncle Kirk's hospital room. How could I turn that down? Still, I thought we'd figure it out. But when I saw you at the art showcase, when I witnessed you thriving and happy and flourishing, I felt like I'd just hold you back. I was about to take an offer from a mid-level team for some decent playing time and a paycheck, but it would have scooped out my soul. The Serpents don't give a shit about me, not like the Bolts." He frowns. "Your world seems so pure. It's lit up with passion and light and energy. And at that moment, mine seemed so fucking bleak. I didn't want to hold you back. And how can I be with you and not be my best?"

The heartache in his voice breaks mine. I stare at Cole and while he's a big, strong, tough hockey player, he's also a scared, uncertain, striving man who's never been protected.

His whole life has been a series of challenges to prove his worth. To live up to a steep personal expectation. To defy the odds.

And when he faltered, he folded. "You should have talked to me. I've been worrying about you for weeks. It seemed like every time I tried to support you, you put up a wall."

"I know. I'm not good at letting people in."

"And I'm not good at pushing. I wish I tried harder to understand you, Cole. For so long, my brothers have protected and sheltered me. I've never been the one worrying and anticipating and reacting. It's probably why I missed the signs with Jay. But I don't want to miss signs with you. How can I know that you're hurting or struggling if you don't reach for me?"

"You can't," he admits.

"How can I trust that you won't do this again?" I gesture toward him. "That things won't overwhelm you and you'll pull away, shut down?"

He takes my hand. "Do it with me."

"What?" I raise my eyebrows.

"Do life with me, Bea. Be my girlfriend. I love you so damn much. I can't promise I won't fuck up again, I can only swear, up and down, that I'll always try. Try to confide in you, try to be a better man, try to be the partner you deserve. I know I won't always get it right, but I want to do it with you."

Tears prick the corners of my eyes. Cole is sincere. He's pouring everything out to me, being as honest as he can. I clear my throat. "My car comes in fifteen minutes. Maybe we should take the next four months to—"

"Please," his voice cracks. "Don't be me. Don't do what I did and shut me out."

His words pull me up short because having suffered on the other end of being iced out, I wouldn't want to do that to anyone, least of all him.

"I'll be busy, Cole. I can't even take phone calls and—"

"I'll write you letters."

"What?" I snort. Is he serious?

"I made you something." He places a small gift bag I assumed was something for Gran on my lap.

"What's this?"

"Open it."

I pull out two clunky mugs. One is blue and green with a "C" stamped in the center. The other is purple and yellow with a "B." I grin, gripping the handles. They're clearly made with love. "You made us his and her mugs?"

"Even though we'll be apart, we can have morning coffee together." He smirks. "You can know, every time you drink out of that mug, that I'm drinking out of it too. And I'm thinking of you, counting the days until you get home." He reaches into his pocket and pulls out a small pouch. Opening it, he pours the contents into my hand. It's a small, delicate necklace with a bumblebee pendant.

"It's beautiful," I whisper, watching the bee flutter in the wind.

"Come home to me, Bea."

I stare at him, losing myself in his eyes and swimming straight to his soul. As much as his breaking up with me hurt, I know he's trying to win me back. I hate being vulnerable but then again, so does Cole. "You'll really write to me?"

"Every week."

"And drink coffee from this mug?" I shake the "C" mug at him.

He takes it and holds it against his chest. "Every morning."

"And do better to communicate?"

"I swear it."

My heart gallops, my fingers feel restless. I love Cole Philips and I *want* to trust him. I *want* to forgive him. For years, I've been trying to get Celine and Beau to hear each other out, to give each other some grace.

Can I do that with Cole? Can I give him another chance?

Pulling his shirt, I press my mouth against his. The moment our lips touch, all the hurt and pain and uncertainty takes a back seat. I feel Cole's apology in the pressure of his mouth. I taste his pain and swallow it. I nibble at our combined fear over an uncertain future. But Cole was right; all we can do is try.

I pull away, our foreheads pressed together.

"Is that a yes?" he pants.

"I love you, Cole Philips. It's a yes."

The biggest smile I've ever seen crosses his face. He kisses me again, his fingers lacing in my hair, his nose pressing against mine.

"I promise to be better at this, Bea."

"Just be you. If you're you and I'm me, we can figure us out."

He nods, kissing me gently. "I miss us."

I smile. "Me too, Cole."

The car the program sent to collect me eases into Gran's driveway.

Blake and Gran step out onto the porch.

Blake slow claps while Gran does a little dance. "It was my sweet tea that made you come back, wasn't it, Cole?"

Cole chuckles and stands. He shakes Blake's hand and kisses Gran's cheek. "Sweetest tea I ever had."

"Secret recipe," Gran teases him.

As I hug Blake goodbye, Beau's car rolls to a stop. "I didn't miss you!" he shouts, getting out of the car and running toward me.

Beau hugs me tight. Then, he smacks Cole's shoulder. "She gave you a second chance?"

Cole nods. "I'm a lucky man."

"Don't fuck it up," Beau warns.

I snort and hug Gran goodbye. My family remains on the porch while Cole picks up my suitcase and places it into the trunk of the waiting car.

I introduce myself to the driver. Then, I round the car and meet Cole for one last kiss goodbye.

"I'll see you in four months," I say.

He tucks a curl behind my ear. "Four months is nothing compared to the future I've got planned for us, Bea."

"Oh, yeah?" I quirk an eyebrow. "You're feeling pretty cocky for a guy who sat on Gran's porch for four hours this morning."

He laughs. "Not cocky, babe. Just confident. I know what I did wrong, and I won't make the same mistake twice."

I cross my arms over my chest. "What, exactly, was the mistake?"

He sobers, his eyes holding mine. "Thinking I could do life without you. Maybe I can but I sure as hell don't want to. You're it for me, Bea. The love of my life."

I smile, my heart feeling a million times lighter than it did this morning. I guess I'll have to pour love into my sculpting now that heartbreak is off the table. The thought makes me chuckle and I wrap my arms around Cole, squeezing him tightly. "And you're mine."

TWENTY-SIX
COLE

OVER THE NEXT FOUR MONTHS

DEAR BEA,

I already miss you! It's hard to think we'll be pen pals for the next four months, but I'm looking forward to your letters the way I used to look forward to a new pair of skates. With massive anticipation. In the meantime: How does a penguin build its house?

The Bolts have been training hard and playing well. We qualified for the play-offs! I'm trying to stay positive, keep my head down, and play my best every game.

I've also been thinking about a lot of the things you said. Your concerns about me putting up a wall and shutting you out. It's something I've heard before—mostly from Jaime. But when you said it, it kind of clicked. At (ready to have your mind blown?) the suggestion of Patton, I sat down and talked to Coach Scotch.

Talking with Coach helped clarify some of the things on my mind. He set me up to talk to one of the team's therapists next week. I'm not going in with expectations. I just want to hear her out, talk some things through, and see what comes of it. Nothing to lose by having a conversation, right?

How's all in your art world? I'm so damn proud of you, my lioness. Can't wait to hear what projects you're working on.

Love, Cole

. . .

DEAR COLE,

Great game last night! I even wrangled my dorm-mates into watching. One of the girls—she's from Texas—had never seen a hockey game before. I'm converting them one by one. You're welcome!

I miss you loads. But, not going to lie, I kind of like the pen pal thing. It's romantic and old-fashioned. Whimsical. And sweet—especially with a joke! I don't know the answer to your joke so please put me and my dorm-mates out of our misery. How does a penguin build its house?

I'm proud of you for talking to Coach! That's huge, Cole. I'm really happy you're seeking support to help clarify things in your head. It seems like you've never let anyone in before and hopefully this therapist can help you balance things out. It's also good for your coaches to know how hard you're grinding. The last thing anyone wants is for you to burn out. Don't push too hard, baby. I love you despite your hockey status! How did your first session go?

Things here are incredible! I'm learning so much. The program is rigorous—all art, all the time. But the mentoring is great. The instructors are very hands-on and invested in our projects, successes, and future goals. It's really made me consider my business plan and the feasibility of opening a shop. I want it, Cole. Badly. I just need to make it happen.

Any tips?

Love you, Bea

DEAR BEA,

Igloos it together. Get it, penguin, igloo?! Funny, right?

Ahh, I'll always be in your corner. I love hearing that you're enjoying your program and getting such great advice. If you want your shop, you'll make it happen. My biggest tip is to always bet on yourself. Any ideas or timeline yet?

I love knowing you and your new friends are tuning into the games. While it was an incredible season, we didn't qualify for the Second Round. Strangely, I'm not as disappointed as I thought I'd be. I think it's because the therapist, Cassie, has been helping me put things in perspective. We're working on new schedules that help balance out my workouts and nutrition in a more constructive, less obsessive way. It's been good for me. So has volunteering.

At Cassie's suggestion, I've started volunteering at a Youth Drug Rehabilitation Clinic. These kids, Bea. Some of them are the strongest people I've ever met. Their stories will wreck you, but they're so damn resilient. Working with them is an honor and I think I'm learning a lot more from them than they are from me. I'm going to up my hours during the summer months. Cut back on the workouts and conditioning and spend more time volunteering. I'll let you know how it goes.

Tell me your favorite thing about your program so far.

And what do you call a belt made of watches?

Thinking of you day and night, Cole

DEAR COLE,

Another joke?! They make my day (almost as much as your letters) because they remind me of when we started dating. Even though we've been apart, I feel closer to you than ever. Thank you so much for the care package. I loved the coffee brews you included as well as the bumblebee socks. Those bath bombs caused a stir in the dorm—everyone is obsessed. Also, thanks for giving Noelle my address. She sent Primrose cupcakes! Between the bath bombs and the sweets, I'm the most popular woman here!

I'm sorry about not making the Second Round. The Bolts had an amazing first season and I'm excited to see what you all achieve next season and in the future. Big things are waiting, baby.

How's everything going at the clinic? That's great that you're connecting with younger kids who may have similar childhoods as you. I'm proud of you for reallocating your time and making their, and your, health such a big priority. I can't wait to hear more about it!

How are your sessions with Cassie going? How is pre-training?

My favorite thing so far is the people! I've linked up with two female potters. We all have different styles but—wait for it!— they're from Tennessee too! We've been discussing opening a store together for the three of us to sell our pottery. It will be a pottery haven but with a wide selection of products in different styles. This way, we can split the expenses, pool our networking and resources, and learn together. What do you think? I'm more than pumped about it.

I made you this little hockey stick pendant. My hands just shaped it as I was lost in thought the other day—guess who I was daydreaming of? Love you, Cole!

XO, Bea

P.S. Send me the answer to the joke!

DEAR BEA,

I finally did it! I made Beef Wellington and it. Didn't. Burn. In fact, it was incredible! You can even ask Gran—she was my dinner date (aka guinea pig!). Blake had a last-minute Zoom meeting so I swooped in to take Gran dancing. For a guy who skates as much as I do, I'm shockingly ungraceful on the dance floor. But, Bea, your gran's got moves! The entire night was hilarious and made me miss you tons. You would have loved everything about the evening. We need to do it again when you're back.

Wow! I love that you might open a shop with two other potters. That sounds like a win-win and an incredible way to achieve your dream in a shorter time frame than you originally thought. Are you thinking of opening up in Nashville? Knoxville? Somewhere else…

Thank you for the hockey pendant! I love it. It's in my locker at The Honeycomb so I can think of you before every workout and know I'm not pushing myself too hard. Sessions with Cassie have been productive. Don't let anyone tell you therapy isn't work.

Talking about shit from my past has been harder than I thought. Sometimes, I'm emotionally exhausted after a session. I realized that instead of letting myself feel and process things, I used to just hit the weights or go for a run. I guess it was a coping mechanism. While therapy has been intense, it's also cathartic. I'm sticking with the sessions and grateful for my other outlet, the clinic. I got a few of the boys and one girl there into hockey so that's been interesting. Maybe one of them will even play one day if they re-enroll in school.

I'm counting the days until I see you!

Love you, Cole

P.S. A waist of time. HA!

DEAR COLE,

Hahaha! That was a good one.

I'm counting the days too—twenty-seven!

I can't imagine how hard it is to open up about your childhood after keeping it close to the chest for so long. But I agree, it's healthy. I'm proud of you for sticking with the sessions and working through the hard, ugly parts with Cassie. If you ever want to talk about anything, I'm always here. I want to support you the best way I can so whatever you need, I'm in. But if you prefer to not talk about these things outside of your sessions, I get that too. Don't ever feel pressured, Cole. I just want you healthy and happy and thriving.

If you're open to it, I'd love to volunteer (even once!) with you at the clinic. I love that you've introduced the kids to hockey. Everyone needs an outlet, an avenue to turn pain into growth. Speaking of growth, what are your top three goals for the future?

The two potters—Meg and Bree—and I are planning to open a shop in downtown Knoxville! Can you believe it? There's a lot of work to do, but we're all excited and invested. I'm grateful for their friendships. This program has made me feel like I belong for the first time since I finished art school. It's like I've met my people, my tribe, out in the wild and it's reminded me that I'm more than the weird, quirky girl with crazy red curls.

Inspired by your present, I've made a his and her mug series. I work on it every morning while drinking coffee out of my "B" mug and thinking of you. I can't wait to show it to you!

See you in less than a month!

Love, Bea

DEAR BEA,

You did it, baby! Or should I say, we did it? Four months apart and I've never felt closer to you. Or more excited about the future we're going to build.

I miss like you mad, Bea. But reading your letters each week has been the sweetest kind of torture. In hindsight, I think it's good we had this time to slow down and learn more about each other. I think this time apart has only strengthened our connection.

In your last letter, you asked me my top three goals. I don't have a definite time frame—I've learned from you to stop rushing every-thing—but I would like to achieve them all before I hit thirty.

Here you go: 1. Become Captain of the Thunderbolts. 2. Grow a real mustache that makes other men jealous (I hear it's harder than it looks). 3. Marry Bea Turner.

What do you think? What are your top three?

I can't wait to see you next week, experience this new mug collection, and hear more about your plans for our future.

Love,

Cole

I sign my name and fold the letter up. Placing it in the envelope, I seal it and walk across the street to the mailbox. I think Bea will receive it before I pick her up next week.

It's been a long four months without my girl, but a signifi-cant four months. Bea and I learned to slow down and enjoy the journey. We learned more about each other through our letters than we did in conversation. I think it's because we weren't afraid to write down our fears or desires since the other person wasn't sitting beside us, waiting to react.

Through our letters, we let each other into our minds and hearts and deepened the connection that's existed since the beginning.

At the beginning of the year, I met a skittish lioness. I fell in love with her and almost messed it all up. But my lioness learned to roar. When she did, I witnessed her in all her glory. I want to witness her every single day for the rest of my life.

Falling in love with Bea was as natural as existing. Being in love with Bea is a gift. Every day she chooses me is one more day that I've earned her trust, her love, her fire.

In one week, Bea will be home and we'll finally start our future together.

I intend to spend it proving her *right*. Proving that she can trust me, count on me, and need me. Showing her, day after day after day, that no one will ever love her the way I do.

EPILOGUE

BEA

Three Weeks Later

"THIS IS A GREAT LOCATION," Bodhi remarks as he walks through the space.

Meg, Bree, and I never expected to launch a store so quickly after the program, but when this space became available, we jumped on it. We plan to open Humble Bee's in two months and there's a lot of work to do. We need to create themed sections, organize the shelves, and roll out a marketing campaign. We have to finalize branding and our website. At times, it's daunting. But, for the most part, I'm filled with excitement and gratitude for fulfilling this dream.

"We're lucky to have snagged it," Bree agrees, dusting off a shelf and rubbing her palms together.

"We've officially shared that Humble Bee's is opening before Christmas," Meg adds. "So, we need to do about a gazillion things."

"Your opening is going to be sick," Blake laughs. "I already heard people talking about it at the diner—"

"And at Corks," Brody cuts in.

"And at the Coffee Grid," Jamie, Cole's cousin, adds.

"It's going to be something," I say, wrapping my arms around my waist. Leaning back against the solid wall of muscle at my back, I take in the space and smile. I did it. Well, we did it. There's no way I'd be here without the support of Cole, my brothers, and Gran. Without the collaboration with Meg and Bree. Without all the love and light in my life.

Cole wraps his arms over mine and holds me close, pressing a kiss to the top of my head. "Proud of you, my Bea."

I turn in his arms and beam up at him. "And I'm proud of you."

Upon my return, Cole shared that the Rehabilitation Clinic asked him to host a monthly support meeting for kids who are interested in sports. His first meeting was overwhelmingly successful.

I know the turnout surprised him. He signed autographs and posed for selfies. But once the group sat down to talk, he was humbled by the number of kids who stayed and shared their stories. His story of growth and overcoming obstacles is one a lot of the kids relate to. I think connecting with Cole gives them hope the same way connecting with them brings him peace.

Cole leans down and kisses me.

"Seriously?" Blake comments.

I pull back and laugh. Cole stares at me, a smirk playing over his mouth, but he doesn't give my brother another look.

"You think this is bad? Try living in Knoxville," Beau scoffs.

"Yeah, because you and Celine were so much better," Bodhi shoots back.

At the mention of Celine, Beau's features lock down, his eyes shuddering closed.

Bodhi swears under his breath.

"She's filming a movie here," I say gently.

Beau's neck snaps in my direction. "What? When?"

I release a breath. "She just told me two nights ago. She didn't think she'd get the part and—"

"When?"

"They start filming in the fall."

"It's September!" Beau snaps.

I sigh. "She'll be here next week."

Beau shakes his head in disbelief.

"Maybe it's for the best," Cole says. "Maybe it's time for the two of you to mend fences."

"Maybe," he murmurs, noncommittally.

Brody releases a sigh. "We'll worry about Celine next week. Right now, let's celebrate our baby Bea and her friends for their new lease and launching Humble Bee's."

I shoot Brody a grateful look.

"I'll be back for the grand opening." Jamie squeezes my hand. "Dad's trying to come too." We just met two weeks ago and already, she's become a surrogate sister. The two of us clicked and I'm happy she plans to visit more.

I squeeze back. "I can't wait to meet Uncle Kirk."

Blake emerges from the back with two bottles of chilled champagne.

"You're dripping on the floor!" Bree follows behind him with a towel.

Meg laughs and holds up a tray with mugs—his and hers. I cheer.

My brother uncorks the bottles and pours them out.

I shift out of Cole's arms and closer to Beau. "You okay?" I say softly, so only he can hear.

"Yeah, just surprised." He slings an arm around my shoulders. "Today is your day, Bea. I'm proud of you."

"I love you, Beau."

"I know," he says, passing me a mug.

Meg asks Beau a question and I turn back to Cole.

He lifts his mug in my direction and grins. "I see the his and her mugs are a hit."

I laugh. "I'll let you know in a few months."

Cole grins and looks around the space. "This is incredible, Bea."

"You're incredible, Cole."

"This is a big week." He steps closer.

I nod, lifting my chin. "It's just the beginning."

Cole dips down and kisses me hard, until butterflies take flight in my belly and my free hand clutches the material of his shirt.

"Damn straight," he agrees, pulling away.

"To Humble Bee's!" Our group lifts their mugs.

"And to you, Bea," Cole murmurs, winking at me.

Emotion swims in my eyes as I stare at the man whose support means everything. "To *us*, Cole."

"I love you," he mouths.

"I love you," I whisper.

Then, we drink to the future. How beautiful, bright, and bold it beckons.

THANK you for reading Rookie's Regret! I hope you love Cole and Bea as much as I do! If you're intrigued by Damien Barnes and adore romances filled with fake dating, a neighbor-turned-more, and a hesitant hero, dive into Playboy's Reward. Turn the page to start reading!

PLAYBOY'S REWARD
CHAPTER ONE - HARPER

The sound of my keys ricocheting off the little dish on the console table clangs loudly in my empty condo. Not just empty, lonely. My bag slips off my shoulder and thuds on the bare floor.

I sigh, flipping on the foyer lights before locking the door behind me.

I'm grumpy. Exhausted. And hangry as hell.

I kick off my heels on the way to the kitchen and peer into the refrigerator, the light illuminating another type of emptiness.

"I forgot to get groceries," I mutter to myself, shutting the refrigerator door.

Sighing again, just because I feel like it, I uncork a bottle of red wine, pour myself a generous glass, and open the Uber Eats app on my phone.

I scroll through the options. Salads and sandwiches, pizzas and burgers, sushi and…my stomach rumbles. I order the jalapeño poppers and nachos, extra beef, extra guac, extra cheese. And a Coke. I deserve a Coke.

Once my order is confirmed, I drop my phone on the kitchen counter, walk around my condo, flipping on lights and opening the blinds I forgot about this morning in my mad dash to make it out the door on time for work. I enter my bedroom, wriggle out of my pencil skirt and blouse, and toss on some leggings and a baggy T-shirt from college. Pulling my hair up in a high ponytail, I relocate to my living room, grab my wine glass, and sink into my favorite chair, staring out at Downtown Knoxville.

Nearly a year ago, I moved back to Tennessee, only twenty minutes from the town I grew up in, as a result of a job offer I couldn't turn down and my mother's incessant nagging that it's time to come home.

Nearly every weekday since, I've dragged my ass out of bed at the crack of dawn to work out, run, or move my body in some way. In the past eleven months, I've made investments and saved money, donated to animal rescue centers, and started journaling. I have an eleven-year-old pen pal in Thailand. I shop local.

And I've never been lonelier.

I gulp my wine, frustrated that so many nights end like this—me, drinking wine, in my living room, alone. My days at work are fulfilling; I love my job. I love working with the Coyotes franchise. I love football...and men who play football.

But now that I'm working for the team, I've drawn a line in the sand. I'm not hooking up with any of the players. That commitment, along with the hours I'm logging at the office, have made my dating life nonexistent.

But who cares if I haven't dated? I've fantasized about my sexy neighbor who lives on the floor above mine, ahem, the penthouse. Does that count as something? Sometimes, if I crane my neck the right way, I can see him sipping a scotch on his balcony, his easy laughter comforting. More often than not, he's got a hot woman with him but who am I to judge? Instead, I take a cold shower and meditate before bed.

I'm *trying*, dammit.

But I am exhausted of trying so damn hard to fit into my old life as a new woman. I haven't fully let go of the anger, the bitterness, the resentment of my past. Of memories that unfolded in my childhood town, on my parents' front lawn.

I certainly haven't moved on enough from the betrayal to connect with my old, high-school friends. Nor have I put myself out there to forge new friendships with other like-minded, career-oriented women in Knoxville.

Instead, I'm in a rut. I'm pushing myself in all aspects of life except the one that truly matters: community. Right now, I have none and the loneliness of that gnaws at me.

I glare at my bag by the front door, recalling its contents. I blame the envelope inside for my current state.

An invitation to my ten-year high-school reunion.

Ugh. I gulp my wine.

Moving back to Tennessee, even to the city, was agonizing. Would I run into Sean? Does Anna mention me anymore? Does she miss my friendship the way I sometimes miss hers? Does Sean tell the women he dates now that he's a cheater? Do they hear the gossip?

Of course, I could ask Mom for the details of Sean's or Anna's lives. But my childhood crush, turned high-school sweetheart, turned college love cheating on me with my forever best friend, cultivating a relationship with her behind my back the semester I studied abroad, announcing that he was marrying her when I returned home, gutted me from the inside out.

They called their wedding off two months before she walked down the aisle and even that didn't provide the vindication I wanted. I don't know if anything ever will.

Their betrayal leveled me, and the scars of their manipulation and lies pushed me from Tennessee to Chicago for six years. Until the job offer—Creative Director of Marketing with THE Knoxville Coyotes, the pride and joy of Southern football—coincided with one of Mom's begging sessions and I caved.

I moved back. I threw myself into work and bettering myself and growing stronger. I've made a hell of a lot of progress too. But that invitation is my undoing.

I polish off my wine and pour another glass.

This is just a weak moment. It won't last. I can wallow in wine and guac tonight and snap back tomorrow. I'll run an extra mile in the morning. The lights outside my window blur and fuck, am I crying?

Swiping a hand over my cheek confirms that I am. I tip my head back and stare at the ceiling instead, willing the tears to reabsorb into my eyeballs. I don't want to be weak. I don't want to care this much. I want to move on and embrace the kick-ass life I'm building for myself in a city that I've loved my whole life.

Besides, I could just not go and save myself the stress, the heartache, the hurt of showing up solo. Because everyone in my town bet that Sean and I would end up together. We were the golden couple—football quarterback and dance team captain, prom king and queen. Anna Drew stabbing me in the back was a plot twist no one saw coming but the town ate it up like handfuls of popcorn during an intense drama. Or, in my case, a psychological thriller.

Yeah, I'm not going. See, that was easy. Decision made.

I release the breath I've been holding. I'm being dramatic and I know it but…can't I give into self-pity tonight? While Mom knows how hard the loss hit me, she doesn't know how much hurt I still drown in. My college friends know Sean and Anna's engagement sent me spiraling, but no one realizes how deep I've sunk.

It's been years. I should be over it. I should be thriving. And most days, I'm faking it enough to believe it. But not tonight. No, tonight proved I'm not ready to see them, and so I will decline the invitation. The people I *want* to talk to from high school, I keep in touch with. One of my old acquaintances, Leo, just signed with the Coyotes and is back in town. We had coffee the other day. Why do I have to see anyone else, when I haven't bothered to reach out to them in the past five years?

I don't. I'm done compromising pieces of myself to fit in, to adapt to anyone's version of who I *should* be. I'm just me and that needs to be enough.

The shrill ring of my phone interrupts my thoughts and I force myself to stand from the chair and dig around my purse.

"Of course," I murmur when I see Mom's name on the screen. "Hello?"

"Harper, you didn't call."

"I just got home thirty minutes ago." A knock sounds on the door and I cradle the phone between my shoulder and cheek as I gratefully accept dinner from the Uber Eats delivery guy.

Mom clucks her tongue. "Working this late? If you could just settle down with a good man, you wouldn't have—"

"I love my job," I cut her off. Working for the Coyotes is a dream come true. My passion for football started long before my romance with Sean. It was born out of my Dad's love for the game and even though I lost Sean, I kept football.

"I know," Mom mutters. "What?" she calls out and I smirk, knowing she's fielding one of Dad's questions. "Your father wants to know how many season tickets you get this year."

I laugh. "I already told him, still two. And we have the whole summer to discuss next season."

Mom chuckles with me. "You know how he is."

"Obsessed."

"Proud," she corrects me, and I grin. When I took the job with the Coyotes, it's possible Dad was more excited than me.

"Thanks, Mom. So, what's going on?" I sink down to the

floor, set the poppers and nachos on the coffee table, and dig in.

Mom's quiet for a long moment and my stomach sinks because I know what's coming.

I open my mouth, but she beats me to it.

"Your high-school reunion is in two weeks," she feigns casual, but I know that she knows exactly what she's doing.

"I'm not going," I blurt out. Rip off that Band-Aid.

"Harper June—"

"Don't middle name me. I'm an adult. If I decide I don't want to see anyone I graduated with, it's—"

Mom's scoffing halts me. "Anyone? Or two specific people?"

"Mom," I groan. "I'm not ready."

"Harper, you live here now. You're going to run into them eventually. Wouldn't it be better to get it over with? You're all adults now…maybe you can find some closure."

"Closure," I mutter. What the hell is that? "I don't want to go," I say firmly.

"I RSVP'd for you," Mom announces, guilt threading her tone.

My heart rate spikes, and a shudder runs through me. "Mom!"

"Harper, it's time. You have your dream job in your dream city near your family. You can't avoid Sean and Anna—"

I blanche at the sound of their names spoken aloud and together.

"Forever," Mom carries on, ignoring my gagging. "At least at the reunion, you have your other friends to lean on. It won't catch you off guard. And you can move on. Come home more, not just counting Sunday dinners. Truly live here, in Knoxville, and spend time with your family and friends without looking over your shoulder."

"Who did you tell I'm going?"

"Karen Drew."

I squeeze my eyes shut. Of course Anna's mom is part of the organizing committee. She was always a super involved parent—Class Mom, Head of the PTA, Organizer for Football Boosters.

"She asked if you're bringing a date," Mom adds and my eyes pop open.

I hold my breath, fearful of Mom's response. What's worse? Going stag or going with a date I beg to accompany me?

Who would I even ask?

Jeremiah pops into my mind. He'd have to drive up from Atlanta, and take off work, but I know he'd do it. Because he's still hoping that something will develop between us, even though we haven't had sex in over five months. Damn, I can't ask him and give him mixed signals.

A few of the single guys on the Coyotes would do me a solid, but that would cause so much speculation that...no, I drew the line in the sand! I can't mix my professional life with my in-shambles personal one.

"I said yes," Mom announces, a quiet indignation in her tone.

It makes me smile, knowing that Mom is on my side. She may be trying to tough love me but deep down, she hates what Sean and Anna did.

"So bring someone sexy," she demands.

I choke on my wine.

Mom snorts. "It's time, Harper. You can do this."

I continue my coughing and drain my second glass. "I don't want to."

"I know. But sometimes, we have to do things we don't want to do. It's called growing up."

"It sucks."

Mom laughs. "I love you, Harp. Let me know if you want to go dress shopping together."

I roll my eyes and exchange good nights with my mom.

Then, I chug another glass of wine, enjoying the numbness that spreads through my body. Except it gives way to hurt when I dig the invitation out of my bag. My hurt morphs into anger at the way Sean and Anna treated me.

And, fuck, besides Jeremiah who will end up being too complicated of a date, what sexy man can I bring as a plus-one?

My dating pool is so shallow, it's pretty much dried up.

Pouring my fourth glass of wine, I stalk out to my balcony, the humid heat hitting my cheeks.

I grip the railing and stare out at the city lights.

Then, I open my mouth and scream.

"Fucking motherfuckerrrrrrrrr!"

ACKNOWLEDGMENTS

Thank you for sharing your time with Bea and Cole! I hope you loved this sweet couple and their hard earned HEA!

As always, all my thanks to the amazing women I'm lucky to work with:

Melissa Panio-Peterson, Amy Parsons, Erica Russikoff, Becca Mysoor, Dani Sanchez and the Wildfire Team, Virginia Carey, the wonderful women of Give Me Books Promotions, Sheila, and Amber — I am so thankful for your encouragement, support, and friendship.

For the covers of this series, I had the great joy of working with Niagara-based photographer Stephanie Iannacchino (www.stecchinoo.com) and these fantastic athletes, and now, cover models: Justin, Manny, Evan, Brady, and Tony. Thank you for collaborating on this project with me!

Infinite thank you's to the bloggers, early reviewers, bookstagrammers, booktokkers, YouTubers, and romance readers everywhere for taking a chance on my books and loving on this new series!

My home team — love you forever.

ALSO BY GINA AZZI

Knoxville Coyotes Football:

Faked and Fumbled

Surprised and Sacked

Trapped and Tackled

The Burnt Clovers Trilogy:

Rebellious Rockstar

Resentful Rockstar

Restless Rockstar

Tennessee Thunderbolts:

Hot Shot's Mistake

Brawler's Weakness

Rookie's Regret

Playboy's Reward

Hero's Risk

Bad Boy's Downfall

Lock 'Em Down

Boston Hawks Hockey:

The Sweet Talker

The Risk Taker

The Faker

The Rule Maker

The Defender

The Heart Chaser

The Trailblazer

The Hustler

The Score Keeper

Second Chance Chicago Series:

Broken Lies

Twisted Truths

Saving My Soul

Healing My Heart

The Kane Brothers Series:

Rescuing Broken (Jax's Story)

Recovering Beauty (Carter's Story)

Reclaiming Brave (Denver's Story)

My Christmas Wish

(A Kane Family Christmas

+ *One Last Chance* FREE prequel)

Finding Love in Scotland Series:

My Christmas Wish

(A Kane Family Christmas

+ *One Last Chance* FREE prequel)

One Last Chance (Daisy and Finn)

This Time Around (Aaron and Everly)

One Great Love

The College Pact Series:

The Last First Game (Lila's Story)

Kiss Me Goodnight in Rome (Mia's Story)

All the While (Maura's Story)

Me + You (Emma's Story)

Standalone

Corner of Ocean and Bay